Marx Joyce
Hardy Machiavelli Chesterton Emerson Austen
Defoe Abbott Montaigne Cooper Hugo
Melville Haggard Eliot Grimm
Stoker Carroll Christie Molière
Wilde Maupassant Byron Schiller
Garnett Einstein Fitzgerald Engels Smith Kafka
Goethe Hawthorne Hall
Cotton Dostoyevsky Willis
Baum Henry Kipling Doyle
Leslie Dumas Nietzsche
Flaubert Turgenev Balzac
Stockton Vatsyayana Crane
Burroughs Verne
Curtis Tocqueville Whitman Gogol Vinci
Homer Widger Tolstoy Busch
Darwin Thoreau Twain Scott
Potter Freud Zola Lawrence Plato Harte
Kant Jowett Stevenson Dickens Hesse
Andersen Burton
London Descartes Cervantes
Poe Aristotle Wells Voltaire Cooke
Hale James Hastings
Bunner Shakespeare Irving
Richter Chambers
Doré Dante da Shaw Benedict Alcott
Swift Chekhov Pushkin
Wodehouse Newton

 **tredition®**

tredition was established in 2006 by Sandra Latusseck and Soenke Schulz. Based in Hamburg, Germany, tredition offers publishing solutions to authors and publishing houses, combined with world-wide distribution of printed and digital book content. tredition is uniquely positioned to enable authors and publishing houses to create books on their own terms and without conventional manufacturing risks.

For more information please visit: www.tredition.com

TREDITION CLASSICS

This book is part of the TREDITION CLASSICS series. The creators of this series are united by passion for literature and driven by the intention of making all public domain books available in printed format again - worldwide. Most TREDITION CLASSICS titles have been out of print and off the bookstore shelves for decades. At tredition we believe that a great book never goes out of style and that its value is eternal. Several mostly non-profit literature projects provide content to tredition. To support their good work, tredition donates a portion of the proceeds from each sold copy. As a reader of a TREDITION CLASSICS book, you support our mission to save many of the amazing works of world literature from oblivion. See all available books at www.tredition.com.

Project Gutenberg

The content for this book has been graciously provided by Project Gutenberg. Project Gutenberg is a non-profit organization founded by Michael Hart in 1971 at the University of Illinois. The mission of Project Gutenberg is simple: To encourage the creation and distribution of eBooks. Project Gutenberg is the first and largest collection of public domain eBooks.

Nero

Stephen Phillips

Imprint

This book is part of TREDITION CLASSICS

Author: Stephen Phillips
Cover design: Buchgut, Berlin – Germany

Publisher: tredition GmbH, Hamburg - Germany
ISBN: 978-3-8472-1465-6

www.tredition.com
www.tredition.de

NERO

by

STEPHEN PHILLIPS

Author of "The Sin of David"

London
MacMillan and Co., Limited
New York: The MacMillan Company
1906

CHARACTERS

NERO . . . . *Emperor of Rome.*

BRITANNICUS . . . . *Nero's Half-Brother.*

OTHO . . . . *A Young Noble.*

SENECA . . . .)) BURRUS . . . .)) *Ministers of State.* TIGELLINUS . . . .)) ANICETUS . . . .)

A SEAMAN.

PARTHIAN CHIEF.

BRITISH CHIEF.

XENOPHON . . . . *A Physician.*

SLAVE TO NERO.

AGRIPPINA . . . . *Nero's Mother.*

OCTAVIA . . . . *Sister to Britannicus.*

POPPAEA . . . . *Wife to Otho, afterwards to Nero.*

ACTE . . . . *A Captive Princess.*

LOCUSTA . . . . *A Poisoner.*

MYRRHA . . . . *Maid to Poppaea.*

HANDMAIDENS, SPIES, ETC.

Five years elapse between Acts I. and II., two years between Acts III. and IV.

ACT I

SCENE. — *The scene is in the Great Hall in the Palace of the Caesars. At the back are steps leading to a platform with balustrade opening on the air, and beyond, a view of the city.*

[*On the right of the stage is a cedarn couch on which* CLAUDIUS *is uneasily sleeping. On the right is a door communicating with the inner apartments. On the left a door communicating with the outer halls.*

[XENOPHON *is standing by the couch of* CLAUDIUS. AGRIPPINA *is sitting with face turned to an* ASTROLOGER, *who stands at the top of the steps watching the stars.*

[LOCUSTA *is crouching beside a pillar, right. A meteor strikes across the sky. The* ASTROLOGER, *pointing upwards, comes down the steps slowly.*

ASTROLOGER. These meteors flame the dazzling doom of kings.

[AGRIPPINA *rises apprehensively.*

XENOPHON. Caesar is dead!

AGRIPPINA. The drug hath found his heart.
  [*To* LOCUSTA, *who steals forward.*
  Locusta, take your price and steal away!
  Sound on the trumpet. Go! your part is done.

[*Exit* LOCUSTA.
[*Trumpet is sounded.*

That gives the sign to the Praetorians
Upon the instant of the Emperor's death.

  [*Answering trumpets are heard.*

Hark! trumpets answering through all the city.
Xenophon, you and I are in this death
Eternally bound. This husband have I slain

To lift unto the windy chair of the world
Nero, my son. Your silence I will buy
With endless riches; but a hint divulged — —

　XENOPHON. O Agrippina, Empress, fear not me!

AGRIPPINA. Meantime his child, his heir, Britannicus,
　Must not be seen lest he be clamoured for.
　So till the sad Chaldean give the sign
　Of that so yearned for, favourable hour,
　When with good omens may my son succeed,
　The sudden death of Claudius must be hid!
　Then on the instant Nero be proclaimed
　And Rome awake on an accomplished deed.

XENOPHON. Then summon Claudius' musicians in
　To play unto the dead as though he breathed.

　AGRIPPINA. Call them! A lulling music let them bring.

[*Exit* XENOPHON.
[*She turns to* ASTROLOGER.

O thou who readest all the scroll of the sky,
Stands it so sure Nero my son shall reign?

　ASTROLOGER. Nero shall reign.

AGRIPPINA. What lurks behind these words?
　There is a 'but' still hovering in the stars.

　ASTROLOGER. Nero shall reign.

　AGRIPPINA. The half! I'll know the rest.

　ASTROLOGER. Peer not for peril!

　AGRIPPINA. Peril! His or mine?

　ASTROLOGER. Thine then.

AGRIPPINA. I will know all, however dark.
  Finish what did so splendidly begin.

  ASTROLOGER. Nero shall reign, but he shall kill his mother.

  AGRIPPINA. Kill me, but reign!

  Enter SENECA

SENECA. The trumpet summoned me,
  And I am here.

AGRIPPINA. Seneca! Speak it low!
  Caesar is dead! Nero shall climb the throne.

SENECA. I will not ask the manner of his death.
  In studious ease I have protested much
  Against the violent taking of a life.
  But lost in action I perceive at last
  That they who stand so high can falter not,
  But live beyond the reaches of our blame;
  That public good excuses private guile.

  AGRIPPINA. You, Xenophon and Burrus, stand with me.

  Enter BURRUS, *right. He salutes the corse of* CLAUDIUS

  BURRUS. Obedient to the trumpet-call I come.

AGRIPPINA. Say, Burrus, quickly say, how stands our cause
  With the Praetorians who unmake and make Emperors?

BURRUS. The Praetorians are staunch,
  And they are marching now upon the Palace.

  AGRIPPINA. Will they have Nero?

BURRUS. Yes, and double pay.
  There is a murmuring minority
  Who toss about the name Britannicus.
  These may be feared; let Nero scatter gold
  There where dissension rises—it will cease.

Their signal when they shall surround the Palace,
The gleam of my unsheathed sword to the dawn.

AGRIPPINA. Stand there until I have from him the sign,
  Then let thy sword gleam upward to the dawn.
  [*Turning and pointing to body of* CLAUDIUS.
  That is my work! Also, I must betroth
  Nero unto the young Octavia,
  And with the dead man's daughter mate my son.
  This marriage sets him firmer on the throne,
  And foils the party of Britannicus.
  [*To* BURRUS.] You for the army answerable stand.
  [*To* SENECA.] And, Seneca, I have entrusted Nero's mind
  To you, to point an eaglet to the sun.
  Nero? What does he?

SENECA. Nero knows not yet
  That Claudius is dead. Rome hath not slept,
  But to the torch-lit circus all have run
  To see him victor in a chariot race,
  Whence he is now returning. A night race
  By burning torches is his newest whim.

AGRIPPINA. A torch-lit race! And yet why not? My child
  Should climb all virgin to the throne of the earth,
  Not conscious of spilt blood: and I meantime
  Will sway the deep heart of the mighty world.
  The peril is Britannicus: for Nero,
  Careless of empire, strings but verse to verse.
  How shall this dove attain the eagle cry?

  SENECA. Be not so sure of Nero's harmlessness.

  AGRIPPINA. What do you mean?

SENECA. By me he has been taught,
  And I have watched him. True, the harp, the song,
  The theatre, delight this dreamer: true,
  He lives but in imaginations: yet

Suppose this aesthete made omnipotent,
Feeling there is no bar he cannot break,
Knowing there is no bound he cannot pass;
Might he not then despise the written page,
A petty music, and a puny scene?
Conceive a spectacle not witnessed yet,
When he, an artist in omnipotence,
Uses for colour this red blood of ours,
Composes music out of dreadful cries,
His orchestra our human agonies,
His rhythms lamentations of the ruined,
His poet's fire not circumscribed by words,
But now translated into burning cities,
His scenes the lives of men, their deaths a drama,
His dream the desolation of mankind,
And all this pulsing world his theatre.
[*Steps heard without.*
The dead man's children startled from their sleep!
Britannicus, Octavia, wondering.

AGRIPPINA. Till the auspicious hour he is not dead.

OCTAVIA *and* BRITANNICUS *enter*

OCTAVIA. We could not sleep: father is very sick.
  We fancied every moment that he called us.

BRITANNICUS. And then these meteors full of coming woe — —

OCTAVIA. So brilliant and so silent! O, I fear them.

BRITANNICUS. Is father yet awake? We want to ask him — —

[THEY *approach the couch.* AGRIPPINA *interposes.*

AGRIPPINA. Do not disturb your father for this night.

OCTAVIA. We will not speak, nor make the smallest sound
  To wake him. We must kiss him ere we sleep.

AGRIPPINA. Children, he is in need of some long rest. Go back
to bed: your father sleepeth sound.

BRITANNICUS. I will go in to him, I will—and you
  Are not our mother. By what privilege
  Do you thus interpose yourself between
  A father and his children?

AGRIPPINA. Would you then
  Trouble him, when to sleep is all he asks?

  OCTAVIA. Only a moment! But to see him!

AGRIPPINA. No!
  Come softly back to bed! no—no—this way!
  Britannicus, with the first peer of light
  You shall behold your father; but not now.
  So the physician, Xenophon, enjoined me.
  Now take Octavia's hand—so, both of you.
  [OCTAVIA *holds her face to be kissed.*
  To-night I think I will not kiss you, child.
  Good-night, good-night.

  [*Exit* OCTAVIA *and* BRITANNICUS.

SENECA. How often have I taught
  And written, 'Children shall not be beguiled
  Even for good ends.' And yet, the single lie
  Must, for the general good, be spoken; yet——

  [MUSICIANS *meanwhile have entered, and are playing dreamy
  music.* AGRIPPINA *turns to* ASTROLOGER, *holding out her
  arms.*

  AGRIPPINA. How long till Rome shall greet her Emperor?

  ASTROLOGER. Behold the heavens! The moment!

  [*Exit* ASTROLOGER.

  AGRIPPINA. Give the sign!

[*Sounds of acclamation and cries of 'Nero.'* BURRUS *draws his sword.*

BURRUS. See the Praetorians!

SENECA. Nero returns.

Enter a HERALD *gorgeously dressed, bearing a silver wreath*

MESSENGER. From Nero unto Agrippina greeting!
  He comes a victor from the chariot race.

[*Sounds of acclamation grow louder, the crowd of* NERO'S *friends and satellites pours in: last comes* NERO *dressed as a charioteer.*

AGRIPPINA. [*Touching* CLAUDIUS' *body.*]
  That music be a dirge: Caesar is dead.
  [NERO *pauses wondering.*
  Claudius is dead. Reign thou. Ave Caesar!

[BURRUS *leads* NERO *to back of platform, and addresses the soldiers at back.*

BURRUS. Caesar is dead! Behold Caesar!

[*A great shout of* 'NERO!' 'CAESAR!' *Meanwhile* AGRIPPINA *and* SENECA *are listening close together. Discordant cries are heard of* 'BRITANNICUS!' *A slave or attendant on* NERO *scatters gold in the direction of these discordant cries, which gradually subside, and are lost in one long shout of* 'Nero, Imperator.' NERO *motions for silence.*

NERO. [*Turning to Court.*] Behold this forest of uprisen spears,
  Symbol of might! But I upon that might
  Would not rely. You hail me Emperor —
  Then hail me as an Emperor of peace.
  First, I declare divinest clemency.
  No deaths have I to avenge, no wrath to bribe,
  No desperate followers clamouring for spoil;
  Pardon from me may beautifully fall.

Next, I bestow full liberty of speech;
I will not sway a dumb indignant earth —
Emperor over the unuttered curse.
Were I myself the mark, I will not flinch.
Yet citizens, if freedom of the tongue
I grant, I'd wish less freedom of the feast.
Then all informers who lie life away
I'll heavily chastise; let no man think
With hinted scandal to employ mine ear.
Last, over all my earth be perfect trust,
That every tribe and people, dusk or pale,
Legions extreme and farthest provinces,
May know that this my hand which striketh down
The oppressor and the tyrant from his seat
Shall raise the afflicted and exalt the meek.
And if this burden grow too vast at times,
Then, mother, teach thy son to bear the load.

[*Exit Court.*

AGRIPPINA. [*Rushing to embrace him. He is vested with the purple and laurel wreath. The body of* CLAUDIUS *is borne off. Exit* BURRUS. NERO *comes down.*] Nero, thou art my son!

NERO. To rule the world.
  How heavy is the sceptre of the earth!

AGRIPPINA. [*Coming down.*] Nero, upon this arm behold I clasp
  This amulet. One dawn two murderers
  Despatched to kill thee, stealing to thy bed
  Were frightened by a snake which from beneath
  Thy pillow glided. From that serpent's skin
  I made this charm. Wear it, and thou shalt prosper;
  But lose it, look thou for calamities.

SENECA. [*Prepares to go also.*] You will
    need sleep, sir, for to-morrow's task.

  NERO. [*In terror.*] I am not pale? Not heavy-eyed?

SENECA. No! No!

NERO. An artist, whatsoever mood he rouse
  In others, should himself be ever still.
  Where is a mirror?

SENECA. Sir, one graver word.
  To-morrow when you first shall sit in judgment,
  And set your name unto the scroll of death — —

NERO. [*Gazing at himself in mirror.*] Ah!
  Must I sign death-warrants? Then I wish
  This hand had never learned to write.

SENECA. Dear pupil!

AGRIPPINA. Your pupil now the awful purple wears.
  You tremble but to grasp the pen! But they
  Who dyed it thus, feared not to grip the brand.

NERO. [*Again looking in mirror.*] It is an act to me unbeautiful.
  To scatter joy, not sadness, was I born.

AGRIPPINA. It is an act to you most necessary,
  If you would sit secure where I have set you.
  Now the light things of boyhood, toys of youth,
  Unworthy that stern seat, you must discard.
  Acte, the playmate of those careless hours,
  Henceforth must be forgotten: you shall wed
  A royal consort — young Octavia,
  The child of Claudius, of the imperial line.

SENECA. My peaceful counsel you will not forget.

NERO. [*Turning to SENECA, affectionately.*]
  Old friend, I am not like to wade in blood,
  Thee at my side! I think upon the dooms
  Of Julius, Caius, and Tiberius,
  All Emperors — all miserably slain.

SENECA. This dawn art thou the master of the world;
  Then tremble at the task to thee assigned.
  Meekly receive the purple and the wreath,
  And on thy knees accept omnipotence.
  Good-night, dear pupil! May my teaching lead
  Thy solemn opportunity aright!

    [*Exit* SENECA.

NERO. You powers sustain me to endure this weight!
  Mother, I shall go mad!

AGRIPPINA. Not while this hand
  Is on thy brow, and this voice in thine ear.

    NERO. To rule the world!

    AGRIPPINA. We two will rule the world.

    NERO. We two?

    AGRIPPINA. When you have need of me, then call me.

NERO. I ever shall. I need you at this moment
  More even than when my toothless gums did fumble
  About thy breast in darkness of the night.

AGRIPPINA. My dear, dear son! And
  Nero, well I know
  That you could never hurt or injure me.
  But you will not forget who set you here—
  You will not, tell me?

    NERO. Never, mother, never!

AGRIPPINA. Mothers for children have dared much, and more
  Have suffered; but what mother hath so scarred
  Her soul for the dear fruit of her body as I?
  Thy birth-pang was the least of all the throes
  That I for thee have suffered—a brief pain,
  A little, little pain we share with creatures;

But what was this to torments of the mind,
The dark, imperial meditations,
Musing with eyes half-closed in moonless night;
The crimes—yes, crimes, the blood that has been spilt—
Why, I have made a way for thee through ghosts.
Nero, you'll not forget?

NERO. Ah! Never, never!

AGRIPPINA. My son, this very night it was foretold
'Nero shall reign, but he shall kill his mother.'
Tell me the stars have lied.

NERO. [*Smiling.*] The stars have lied.

Enter BURRUS

BURRUS. The pass-word, sir, to-night?

NERO. The best of mothers.

AGRIPPINA. Kiss me; we both of us must sleep awhile.

[*Exit* AGRIPPINA. NERO *goes up, gazing out on the city as the
dawn comes on greyly.*

NERO. O, all the earth to-night into these hands
Committed! I bow down beneath the load,
Empurpled in a lone omnipotence.
My softest whisper thunders in the sky,
And in my frown the temples sway and reel,
And the utmost isles are anguished. I but raise
An eyelid, and a continent shall cower;
My finger makes the city a solitude,
The murmuring metropolis a silence,
And kingdoms pine in my dispeopling nod.
I can dispearl the sea, a province wear
Upon my little finger; all the winds
Are busy blowing odours in mine eyes,
And I am wrapt in glory by the sun,
And I am lit by splendours of the moon,
And diadem'd by glittering midnight.

O wine of the world, the odour and gold of it!
There is no thirst which I may not assuage;
There is no hunger which I may not sate;
Nought is forbidden me under heaven!
[*With a cry.*] I shall go mad! I shall go mad!

[ACTE *steals in noiselessly, and waits till he turns, then
comes down to him.*

My Acte!

ACTE. [*Shrinking.*] O, I seem so far from you,
  And so beneath you now; your care henceforth
  The world and nothing less. Long have you been
  Nero to me, but Caesar must be now
  High throned, the nations crawling at your feet.
  And yet be sure that if on some far day
  The throne should pass from you; if you should stand
  Lonely at last; your friends all fallen away
  From you; the laurel upon other brows
  Set; were you dyed in blood deep as the robe
  That folds you; were you dead in rags reposing,
  Yet would I find you, cover up your face,
  Taking the last kiss from your lips, and I
  Would gently bury you within the earth.

  NERO. Ah!

ACTE. And though none came nigh you, being dead,
  Who were in life so thronged about and pressed,
  One hand at least would duly pluck you flowers,
  One hand at least would strew them on your grave.
  Sleep now, and I will charm these eyes to close.

[*She takes a harp, and as she plays* NERO *drops off to sleep. She,
seeing him so, softly kisses him and noiselessly disappears. Meanwhile* NERO *turns uneasily in his sleep, and a procession of dead
Emperors passes* — JULIUS, *covering his face, but withdrawing his
cloak to gaze a while on* NERO; TIBERIUS; CAIUS *wounded;*

CLAUDIUS *holding a cup.* NERO *rushes forward, uttering a cry.*
ACTE *again re-enters at the sound.*

Nero, what ails you? Nero, how the drops
Stand on your brow!

NERO. There, there, I seemed to see
  As in procession the dead Emperors:
  Julius, Tiberius, Caius, Claudius,
  All bloody, and all pacing that same path.

ACTE. [*Trying to lead him on the opposite way.*]
  There is another path, will you but take it.

  [NERO *is led by her a little way, then hesitates, still gazing after
  the procession of Emperors. Gradually he looses* ACTE'S *hand, and
  she leaves him, gazing.*

ACT II

SCENE.—*The same, but signs of excessive luxury and profusion. Rich carpets, gilded pillars, etc. As the scene opens, strange oriental music is heard, with singing.* **GIRLS** *enter slowly and place wreaths round the various statues of* **NERO**, *who is depicted now as Apollo singing, now as a charioteer.*

[ACTE *is reclining on a couch. The time is broad noon. A faint exotic odour pervades the palace.*

1ST MAIDEN. O Lydia, I am drowsing, and my hands
  Can scarcely wreathe the Emperor as Apollo.

2ND MAIDEN. Ah, crown this carefully!
  To-day he sings
  In public; as Apollo will return
  So crowned, so garbed.

  1ST MAIDEN. How is that wreath disposed?

  2ND MAIDEN. Excellent!

  3RD MAIDEN. O please tell me how to droop These scarlet flowers.

  2ND MAIDEN. About the lyre then, thus.

  4TH MAIDEN. This bust now of the Emperor as a boy?

  1ST MAIDEN. O, covered with white flowers and birds of spring.

  5TH MAIDEN. This charioteer: with green I have dressed that.

  3RD MAIDEN. Yes, for the Emperor's colour is the green.

  1ST MAIDEN. Now all the busts are wreathed.

  2ND MAIDEN. What more to do?

  1ST MAIDEN. All is arranged. How heavy are my eyes.

3RD MAIDEN. And this low music on my spirit hangs.

4TH MAIDEN. And the faint odour steals upon my hair.

1ST MAIDEN. [*Moving up and leaning out.*
  See, all the city is a solitude.

2ND MAIDEN. All Rome is gathered in the theatre
  To hear the Emperor sing.

5TH MAIDEN. O, I should sleep
  On such a noon, in such a throng.

1ST MAIDEN. That sleep
  Would have no wakening, if your eyes but closed
  While Caesar sang.

4TH MAIDEN. To-night there is a feast.
  Have you remembered?

3RD MAIDEN. Yes, the dancing girls
  From Egypt are arrived.

1ST MAIDEN. We are to strew
  Down from the ceiling flowers upon the guests.

  [*They recline in various attitudes about the seats and pillars.*

  Enter SENECA *and* BURRUS

BURRUS. Ah, Seneca, five years since Nero climbed
  The throne; and in this very chamber, now
  So changed, this odour — pah! This was the place,
  Grim, bare, for military virtues apt.

SENECA. And he how changed! The boy who dreamed so high
  Of mightiest empire and unmeasured peace,
  All I had taught him lost; by flattery sapped,
  Jewelled and clothed as from the Orient,

He sings and struts with dancers and buffoons.

ACTE. [*Starting up.*] And you, when have you two dissuaded him?
  Or when forbidden? Do you teach him shun
  Languor or luxury? You lure him thither.

SENECA. 'Tis true that we have not dissuaded him,
  But out of high deliberate policy
  Have suffered him to tread the path of folly
  Rather than mischief. We have ruled the world
  With wisdom these five years while he has played.

ACTE. What of Poppaea, Otho's wife. Have you
  Restrained that madness? Rather have you not
  Screened it and fed it?

SENECA. With the same design;
  Better that he should vent his madness thus
  In pastime to the State not perilous,
  Amuse himself with her rather than Rome.

ACTE. A woman without pity, beautiful.
  She makes the earth we tread on false, the heaven
  A merest mist, a vapour. Yet her face
  Is as the face of a child uplifted, pure;
  But plead with lightning rather than those eyes,
  Or earthquake rather than that gentle bosom
  Rising and falling near thy heart. Her voice
  Comes running on the ear as a rivulet;
  Yet if you hearken, you shall hear behind
  The breaking of a sea whose waves are souls
  That break upon a human-crying beach.
  Ever she smileth, yet hath never smiled,
  And in her lovely laughter is no joy.
  Yet hath none fairer strayed into the world,
  Or wandered in more witchery through the air,
  Since she who drew the dreaming keels of Greece
  After her over the Ionian foam.

BURRUS. Better an Emperor fooled than Rome undone!

ACTE. Though all unite to drive him to his doom,
  Yet I will not forsake him till he die.

  [*Exit* ACTE.

    [*Meanwhile there is an uneasy movement among the* GIRLS, *as at
    the approach of something sinister.* TIGELLINUS *enters, gasping.*

  TIGELLINUS. [*Looking after* ACTE.] She is a Christian!

  BURRUS. Tigellinus!

TIGELLINUS. I
  Come from the theatre. For three hours have sat
  In the first bench, and feared to wink or cough.
  The Emperor sang, and had for audience
  The flower of Rome. In torment did we sit,
  Nobles and consuls, captains, senators,
  Bursting to laugh and aching but to smile.
  Higher and higher rose the Emperor's voice,
  But no man ventured to relax his lips.
  And all around were those who peered or crept,
  Inspecting each man's face, noting his look.
  To sigh was treason and to laugh was death,
  And yet none dared be absent: how were you
  Excused?

  BURRUS. I pleaded the old wound.

SENECA. And I
  Reception of the Parthian and the Briton.

TIGELLINUS. I
  Say not so much against his moody freaks,
  But to be called from bed to hear him sing —
  O, I must have my sleep at night — well, well —
  To graver things. Still the conspiracy
  Of Agrippina swells: she aims to make
  Her son a toy, a puppet, while she pulls

Unseen the secret strings of policy.

SENECA. Is't not enough to bear upon her back
  Stripped continents? To clasp about her throat
  A civilisation in a sapphire, or
  That kingdoms gleam and glow upon her brow.
  Now doth she overstar us like the night
  In splendour. Now she rises on our eyes
  Dawning in gold; or like the blaze of noon
  Taketh our breath on a sudden; or she glides
  Silent, from head to foot a glimmering pearl.
  But this is woman's business: 'tis not so
  To listen screened to the ambassadors,
  To ride abroad with Nero charioted,
  Or wear her head upon the public coins.

TIGELLINUS. And she intends this very day to hear
  The Briton, seated by the Emperor's side.
  Otho has joined her too.

  SENECA. But from what cause?

  TIGELLINUS. He is married.

  BURRUS. Ah, Poppaea!

TIGELLINUS. Jealousy
  Hath driven him into Agrippina's snare.
  Fury at Nero's madness for his wife.
  Now what if we could raise Poppaea up
  As Agrippina's chief antagonist:
  We match the mistress 'gainst the mother — pit
  Passion 'gainst gratitude — a sudden lure
  'Gainst old ascendency, the noon of beauty
  Against the evening of authority,
  The luring whisper 'gainst the pleading voice,
  The hand that beckons 'gainst the arm that sways,
  And set a woman to defeat a woman.
  To Nero I have whispered that she dotes
  Upon his poems, on his rhythm hangs,

And cannot sleep for beauty of his verse.

SENECA. This day must Nero leave his mother's lap,
  And stand up as an Emperor, and alone.

  [*Trumpet.*

  BURRUS. Hark! Caesar is returning.

  [*Sounds heard of* NERO *approaching amid cries of 'O thou Apollo!'
'Orpheus come again!' Then enter* NERO *with a group of satellites,* TI-
GELLINUS, OTHO, *and professional applauders and spies. His dress is
of extreme oriental richness, and profuse in jewels: his hair elaborately
curled. He carries an emerald eye-glass, and appears faint from the exertion
of singing, from which contest he has just come.*

NERO. This languor is the penalty the gods
  Exact from those whom they have gifted high.

SENECA. [*Coming forward.*] Sir, late arrived
    from Parthia and Britain — —

NERO. [*Starting up.*] A draught!
  [*Much hurry, zeal, and confusion among courtiers.*
  This kerchief closer round my throat!
  [*They tie a kerchief round his throat.*
  Was I in voice to-day? The prize is won,
  But I would be my own competitor
  And my own rival. Was I then in voice?

CHORUS. O Memnon struck with morning, nightingale,
  Ghost-charming Orpheus, O Apollo — god!

SATELLITE. O Caesar, I am one who speaks right out;
  If it means death, yet must I speak the truth.
  Thy voice was harsh.

  NERO. Was it so, friend?

SATELLITE. Harsh and uncertain. Had it been another
  Who sang, it would have ravished every ear,
  But thee must I remember at thy best,
  And what in others we count excellence
  In thee we count a lapse, and falling off.

  NERO. There's a good fellow!

  SENECA. Caesar!

  NERO. But a moment!

  1ST SPY. [*Stealing forward.*] Licinius smiled, sir, at thy final note.

NERO. Nothing! an artist must bear ridicule.
  Were I incensed, I were ridiculous
  Myself.

  1ST SPY. Shall nothing then be done?

  NERO. Nothing!

  2ND SPY. [*Stealing forward.*] Sir, Labienus, in thy second song
Coughed twice.

  ANOTHER SPY. [*Cringing.*] Nay, Caesar, thrice.

  2ND SPY. What punishment?

NERO. None! Interruption must I learn to bear.
  What patience must we own who would excel!
  Anger I never must permit myself,
  Or ruffling littleness to this great soul.

3RD SPY. [*Creeping forward.*] Sir, Titus
  Cassius yawned while thou didst sing.

  4TH SPY. Nay, Caesar, worse, he slept, and must he live?

NERO. [*Gently.*] No! he must die: there is no hope in sleep.
  Witness, you gods, who sent me on the earth
  To be a joy to men: and witness you
  Who stand around: if ever a small malice

Hath governed me: what critic have I feared?
What rival? Have I used this mighty throne
To baulk opinion or suppress dissent?
Have I not toiled for art, forsworn food, sleep,
And laboured day and night to win the crown,
Lying with weight of lead upon my chest?
Ye gods, there is no rancour in this soul.
  [*Thunder.*
Silence while I am speaking. He must die,
Because he is unmindful of your gifts
And of the golden voice on me bestowed,
To me no credit; and he shall not die
Hopeless, for ere he die I'll sing to him
This night, that he may pass away in music.
How foolish will he peer amid the shades
When Orpheus asks, 'Hast thou heard Nero sing?'
If he must answer 'No!' I would not have him
Arrive ridiculous amid the dead.

  SENECA. Caesar, the Parthian and the British chiefs.

NERO. I cannot, sirs, so suddenly return
  Unto life's dreary business, or descend
  Out of the real to the unreal: from that
  Which is to that which is not. Leave me still.
  From art to empire is too swift a drop.

OTHO. Now what to do? Still drags the o'erlong day.
  We have driven, we have eaten, we have drunk.
  But all the brilliance is a burden still.

ANICETUS. No cloud upon the noon of this despair.
  O for some edge, some thrill unknown!

  LUCAN. Remorse?

  [NERO *shakes his head.*

  SENECA. Jealousy then?

NERO. No, no—we have outlived
  All passions: terror now alone is left us.
  I have within me great capacities
  For terror: fear, the last, the greatest passion!

OTHO. Can one rely on death for something new?
  Some other life perhaps.

SENECA. The gods forbid!
  The Power that sent us here would lead us there.
  One sample is enough.

LUCAN. Death's a dull business,
  Of that one may be sure. What says the poet?
  'When I am dead, let fire devour the world.'

  [NERO *starts at these words and comes among them.*

NERO. Nay, while I live! The sight! A burning world!
  And to be dead and miss it! There's an end
  Of all satiety: such fire imagine!
  Born in some obscure alley of the poor,
  Then leaping to embrace a splendid street,
  Palaces, temples, morsels that but whet
  Her appetite: the eating of huge forests:
  Then with redoubled fury rushing high,
  Smacking her lips over a continent,
  And licking old civilisations up!
  Then in tremendous battle fire and sea
  Joined: and the ending of the mighty sea:
  Then heaven in conflagration, stars like cinders
  Falling in tempest: then the reeling poles
  Crash: and the smouldering firmament subsides,
  And last, this universe a single flame!

  [OTHO, *seeing the steward and musician,*
  who have entered, speaks.

OTHO. Nothing is left us but to eat and drink.

[*Takes bill of fare which the steward passes to him.*

NERO. The feast!

[*Takes bill of fare from* OTHO.

You understand that in the perfect feast
To please the palate only is not art,
But we should minister to the eye and the ear
With colour and with music. Introduce
The embattled oysters with a melody
Of waves that wash a reef — whence do they come?

    STEWARD. From Britain, sir.

NERO. Perhaps an angrier chord
  Of island surf might be permitted then.
  From Britain? Now I see thy uses, Britain.
  Britain is justified: she gives us oysters,
  And therefore Claudius invaded her.
  Sausages upon silver gridirons?

    STEWARD. Yes.

NERO. Dormice with poppies and milk honey? There
  A slumberous music, heavy lingering chords.
  Ah! slices of pomegranate underneath.
  Snow — purest snow of course.

    STEWARD. 'Twas not forgot.

NERO. Then glorying peacocks: here a sounding march,
  Something triumphal — even a trifle loud.
  And, ah! the mullets! You remembered them?

    STEWARD. O Caesar, yes.

NERO. Let these be introduced
  By some low dirge. And let us see them die —
  Slow-dying mullets within crystal bowls,

Dying from colour unto colour: now
Vermilion death-pangs fading into blue —
A scarlet agony in azure ending.
There we have colour! And at last the tongues
Of nightingales — the tongues of nightingales?
O, silence with the tongues of nightingales.

[*He dismisses* STEWARD.]

TIGELLINUS. Sir, grant us three a moment's audience.

[NERO *dismisses friends and satellites with gesture.*

SENECA. Your mother, sir, this very day intends
  To hear the British chiefs in audience,
  Sitting beside you. Know then that the world
  Will not endure to have a woman's rule.

  BURRUS. No, nor the army.

TIGELLINUS. And thy mother laughs
  In public at thy verse.

NERO. She has no ear.
  I pity her — remember what she loses.

TIGELLINUS. Ah, be not laughed at, sir, be it not said
  Nero is tied unto his mother's robe.
  Be brilliant, cruel, lustful, what you will,
  But not a naughty child, rated and slapped.
  Poppaea too, she will not suffer you
  With her to indulge your fancy.

  SENECA. Caesar, rise!

  BURRUS. Rise — rise, and reign!

TIGELLINUS. And be no more a doll
  That dances while she pulls the string behind.
  Then young Britannicus!

NERO. O nothing!

TIGELLINUS. Yet
  He is winning on the people: he hath charm,
  His voice is sweet.

  [NERO *starts.*

  Caesar, I judge it not,
  But speak the common drift; and his recital,
  So I am told, has for accompaniment
  Gesture most eloquent.

  [NERO *is more and more roused.*

  His poems, too!

NERO. [*Breaking the silence.*] His poems!
  Why, why, not a line will scan
  To the true ear; and what variety,
  I ask you all — what flow, or what resource
  Is shown? A safe monotony of rhythm!

  [*He paces to and fro angrily.*

TIGELLINUS. Caesar, I cannot speak to such a theme.
  Merely Rome's mouthpiece.

NERO. And his gesture, why,
  'Tis of the Orient, and gesticulation
  More happily were called; never a stillness,
  Never repose, but one wild whirl of arms.

TIGELLINUS. I spoke not of fulfilment, but of promise,
  The artist's dazzling future.

NERO. A sweet voice!
  Rome hath no critics! I would write a play
  Lived there a single critic fit to judge it.
  Whether a dancing-girl kick high enough —

On this they can pronounce: this is their trade.
With verse upon the stage they cannot cope.
Too well they dine, too heavily, and bear
The undigested peacock to the stalls.

TIGELLINUS. Should Agrippina on a sudden change
  Her front, and clasp hands with Britannicus?

  NERO. Your words awaken in me a new thirst.

  SENECA. Sir, hear the Parthian and the British chiefs.

  NERO. [*Going to the throne.*] Summon them!

  [*Exit* SENECA.

Think not, though my aim is art,
I cannot toy with empire easily.
The great in me does not preclude the less.

  [*Re-enter* SENECA *with* PARTHIAN *and* BRITISH AMBAS-
SADORS, *followed by the Court.* SENECA *brings forward the*
PARTHIAN CHIEFS, *when* AGRIPPINA *enters magnificently
dressed and begins to mount steps of throne.* NERO *with courteous
decision brings her down.*

Mother, this is man's business, not for thee.
You jar the scheme of colour — mar the effect.

PARTHIAN. Caesar, we starve: all Parthia parches: all
  Our crops sun-smitten bleach upon the plains.
  We ask thy aid.

NERO. And ye shall have my aid
  Even to the fullest: further, I will open
  The imperial granaries for your people's wants.

PARTHIAN. Caesar, we thank thee: and if ever thou
  Shouldst need the Parthian aid, whate'er the cost,

That aid thou shalt find ready at thy side.

   [*Exit.*

BRITISH CHIEF. Caesar, the tax that thou hast laid on us
  Remit, we pray thee, else we rise in arms
  And will abide thy battle.

NERO. So! You dream
  That Caesar being merciful is weak.
  I who can succour, I can strike; I'll launch
  The legions over sea, and I myself
  Will lead them, and the eagles will unloose
  Through Britain—I who sit on the world's throne
  Will have no threatening from Briton, Gaul,
  People or tribe inland or ocean-washed.
  The terror of this purple I maintain.
  You are dismissed.

[NERO, *spreading his hands, dismisses the Court, and comes down to his mother.*

  NERO. Now, mother!

AGRIPPINA. I will speak
  With you alone, not compassed by these men.

  [*To* SENECA *and* BURRUS.] To me you owe the height where now you stand. Who took you, schoolmaster, from exile? Who Unstewarded you, Burrus? If I have made, I can unmake—Now leave me with my son. [*To* TIGELLINUS.] You are self-made. Gods! I'd no hand in that!

[*Exeunt* SENECA, BURRUS, *and* TIGELLINUS.]

Nero, have you forgot who set you there?

NERO. Not while I hear it twenty times a day.

AGRIPPINA. You should not need that I remind you of it.

NERO. A kindness harped on grows an injury.

AGRIPPINA. Are you the babe that lay upon my breast?

NERO. I was: but I would not lie there for ever.

AGRIPPINA. Have I not reared you, tended you, and loved you?

NERO. Yes, but to be your puppet and your toy.

AGRIPPINA. Boy, never since I first looked on the sun
  From man or woman had I insolence,
  Who have sistered, wived, and mothered Emperors.

  NERO. I speak no insolence — you weary me!

AGRIPPINA. Gods! you have hit on a new thing to tell me.
  [*Coming to him.*] Does your heart beat? Are
      you all ice and pose?
  Has nothing gripped you — is there aught to grip
  In you, pert shadow? Have you e'er shed tears?

NERO. For legendary sorrows I can weep:
  With those of old time I have suffered much,
  And I, for dreams, am capable of tears;
  But not for woe too near me — and too loud.

AGRIPPINA. O wall of stone 'gainst which I beat in vain!
  Nero, I will do much to win you back
  For your own sake: and though it hurts me sore,
  Your passion for Poppaea I will aid.
  When did a mother yield herself to this?

NERO. When had a mother such a lust for rule
  That she could even yield herself to this?

AGRIPPINA. [*Clasping his knees.*] Child, I
      have done with scorn, with bitter words,
  With taunt, with gibe. Now I ask only pity —
  A little pity from flesh that I conceived,

A little mercy from the body I bore,
And touches from the baby hands I kissed.
Nothing I ask of you, only to love me,
And if not that, to bear with me a while,
Who have borne much for you: no, Nero, child,
I will not weary you, I yearn for you.
Forgive me all the deeds that I have done for you,
Forget the great love I have spent on you,
Pardon the long, long life for you endured.

[NERO *is moved and kisses her, then speaks with effort.*

NERO. Mother, if I have seemed to be forgetful,
  Or cruel even, impute it not to me
  But to the State.

[AGRIPPINA *starts.*

'Tis thought that neither Rome,
The provinces, nor armies, will endure
To see a woman in such eminence.
Therefore it is advised that you retire
To Antium a while, and leave Rome free.

AGRIPPINA. [*Starting up.*] Leave Rome!
  Why, I would die as I did step
  Outside her gates, and glide henceforth a shadow.
  The blood would cease to run in my veins, my heart
  Stop, and my breath subside without her walls.
  All without Rome is darkness: you will not
  Despatch my shadow down to Antium?

  NERO. We were remembering your toils, your age.

AGRIPPINA. My age! Am I old then?
  Look on this face,
  Where am I scarred, who have steered the bark of State
  As it plunged, as it rose over the waves of change?
  I was renewed with salt of such a sea.

Empires and Emperors I have outlived;
A thousand loves and lusts have left no line;
Tremendous fortunes have not touched my hair,
Murder hath left my cheek as the cheek of a babe.

[*At this moment* BURRUS, SENECA, *and* TIGELLINUS *return, hearing the scene; and as* AGRIPPINA *continues her imprecations, the* COURT *return and stand in groups listening.*

AGRIPPINA. My age! Who then accuses me of age?
  Was this a flash from budding Seneca,
  Or the boy Burrus' inspiration? Say?
  Do I owe it to the shrivelled or the maimed?

SENECA. Empress, it is determined you retire.
  And you will better your own dignity
  And his assert, if you will make this going
  To seem a free inclining from yourself.

AGRIPPINA. Bookman, shall I learn policy from you?
  Be patient with me. Nero, you I ask,
  Not schoolmasters or stewards I promoted.
  Is it your will I go to Antium?
  Speak, speak. Be not the mouthpiece of these men:
  Domitius!

  NERO. Mother, 'tis my will you go.

AGRIPPINA. Then, sir, discharge me not from your employ
  Without some written commendation,
  That I can tire the hair or pare the nails,
  That those who were my friends may take me in!

  NERO. Lady!

  AGRIPPINA. O, lady now? Mother, no more!

NERO. [*Pacing fiercely to and fro.*] Beware
    the son you bore: look lest I turn!

Chafe not too far the master of this world.

AGRIPPINA. See the new tiger in the dancer's eye:
  'Ware of him, keepers—then, you bid me go?
      [*A pause.*
  Then I will go. But think not, though I go,
  My spirit shall not pace the palace still.
  I am too bound by guilt unto these walls.
  Still shall you hear a step in dead of night;
  In stillness the long rustle of my robe.
  So long as stand these walls I cannot leave them.
  Yet will I go: behold you, that stand by,
  A mother by her own son thrust away,
  Cast out—ha, ha!—in my old age, infirm,
  To totter and mumble in oblivion!

NERO. [*To* SENECA *and* BURRUS.] A little
      violent that—did you not think so?
  And yet the gesture excellent and strong!

AGRIPPINA. Romans, behold this son: the man of men;
  This harp-player, this actor, this buffoon——

  NERO. Peace!

AGRIPPINA. —sitting where great Julius but aspired
  To sit, and died in the aspiring: see,
  This mime—my son is he? And did I then
  Have one mad moment with a street musician?

  SENECA. Have you no shame?

AGRIPPINA. This son now sends me forth,
  Yet it was I, his mother, set him there.

  [*Murmur.*

And, ah! if it were known at what a price,
Witness, you shades of the Silani!

SENECA. Peace!

AGRIPPINA. And witness Messalina on vain knees!

[*Murmur.*

And witness Claudius with the envenomed cup.

NERO. Silence, or — —

AGRIPPINA. Not the seas shall stop me now,
  Raging on all the shores of all the world.
  Witness if easily my son did reign,
  I am bloody from head to foot for sake of him,
  And for my cub am I incarnadined.

[*Murmur.*

I'll go, but if I fall, Rome too shall fall:
I'll shake this empire till it reel and crash
On that ungrateful head; and if I fall,
The builded world shall tumble down in thunder.

[*Murmur.*

Ah!

[*Seeing* BRITANNICUS.] To my arms, boy! [*Snatches him to her side.*] Tremble now and shake! Here is the true heir to the imperial throne, Deposed by me, but now by me restored.

[*Uproar.*

I'll to the Praetorians!

[*Clamour.*

            To the camp!
And there upon the one side they shall see
Britannicus the child of Claudius,
And me the daughter of Germanicus;
And on the other side a harp-player,

A withered pedant, and a maimèd sergeant,
Disputing for the diadem of the earth.
Come, Caesar, away to the Praetorians!

[*Exit* AGRIPPINA *leading* BRITANNICUS, *followed by*
COURT *in great excitement, all but* BURRUS *and* SENECA, TI-
GELLINUS *and* NERO — *a blank pause.*

SENECA. Now what to do?

TIGELLINUS. Already can I hear
The roar of the Praetorians and their march,
This time to crown another. Burrus, you
Command them.

BURRUS. They would tear me into pieces,
As hounds a master entering in on them
Unrecognised, if Agrippina once
Hallooed to them the name 'Germanicus.'

TIGELLINUS. Surely Britannicus must be our aim:
He gone, what threat, what counter-move hath she?
Removing him, we take the sting from her;
Then let her buzz at will.

BURRUS. But he is gone.

SENECA. Even as an eagle snatches up a babe,
So Agrippina caught him up and flew.

TIGELLINUS. For once my wits are lost.

SENECA. Still, what to do?

[NERO *has been sitting with his back to them, suddenly rises.*

NERO. Leave this to me!

TIGELLINUS. O Caesar!

NERO. [*To* ANICETUS.] Go thou fast
And intercept my mother on her way,

And say thou thus: 'Nero thy son repents
His former ire and cancels the decree
For Antium; and prays thou may'st return
To supper, as a sign of amity,
And bring with thee the prince Britannicus.'

   [ANICETUS *is going, but* NERO *stops him.*

And as you go, send in to me Locusta.

   [*Exit* ANICETUS.

I have conceived — not fully — but conceived
The death-scene of the boy Britannicus.
Leave this to me.

   TIGELLINUS. O Caesar!

NERO. It shall be
Performed to-night at supper: get you seats;
It shall be something new and wonderful,
Done after wine, and under falling roses;
And there shall be suspense in it, and thrill:
It shall be very sudden, very silent,
And terrible in silence — I the while,
Creator and arranger of the scene,
Reclining with a jewel in my eye;
And Agrippina shall be close to me,
Aware, yet motionless: Octavia,
Though but a child, yet too discreet for tears.
This you may deem as yet a little crude,
But other details I will add ere supper.

   [SENECA *withdraws in horror, as do the others, slowly.*

   SENECA. Here's what I feared!

TIGELLINUS. His eyes now! Yet how calm!
So steals the panther, stirring not a leaf!

[*Exeunt slowly* SENECA, TIGELLINUS, *and* BURRUS. NERO
walks to and fro, constructing the scene in pantomime to himself.
LOCUSTA *enters down, right.*

NERO. You are Locusta, and your trade is poison.

[*She makes obeisance.*

[*Uneasily.*] Is poison but a trade with you, or art?
Surely to slay is the supreme of arts;
And with no ugly wound or hideous blow,
But beautifully to extinguish life.
Have you some rare drug that kills suddenly?
As I have planned it, I can have no pause —
Death must be sudden — silent. And my guests
Must not be wearied with a pang prolonged,
And there must be no cry. That understand.

[LOCUSTA, *grovelling at his feet.*

LOCUSTA. O Caesar, such a drug is known to me, —
But I will not reveal it.

NERO. Die then.

LOCUSTA. Die?
O, I love life, but this I'll not reveal.

NERO. Ah, you must live — you are an artist too.

LOCUSTA. I have a poison that is slipped in wine —
Not nauseous to the taste.

NERO. An artist still!
Let me have that, and suddenly. And listen —
The cup presented to Britannicus
Must be too hot: so that he calls for snow
To cool it. In that snow the poison lurks.

[*Exit* LOCUSTA.

[ANICETUS *hastily returns.*

ANICETUS. O Caesar, the Augusta had not left
  The palace; and now, o'erjoyous at thy words,
  She will be present at the supper-board,
  Bringing with her the prince Britannicus.

[*Servants enter with various dishes and arrange the tables and
couches for the guests, and supper begins.*

[*They all recline amid a low hum of conversation. Dreamy music
is heard, which might be a continuation of the music played before.*

NERO *reclines at the head of the central table between* AGRIP-
PINA *and* OCTAVIA. POPPAEA *is a prominent figure.* BRI-
TANNICUS, *with other youths, lies at a side table.* SENECA,
BURRUS, *and* TIGELLINUS *present with other members of the
Court. At a sign from* NERO *dancing girls enter and perform a
strange, wild measure, after which the hum of conversation is re-
sumed. Again, at a sign from* NERO, *odours are spurted over the
guests amid cries of delight.*

[*At a sign from* NERO, *flowers descend from the ceiling. At first
lilies, then of deeper and deeper colour. At last a tempest of roses
which gradually slackens.*

NERO. Britannicus, I voice a general wish.
  Sweet is it, early and thus easily
  To have garnered fame: the crown is for the few,
  And these are tasked to reach it ere they die.
  Oftener the laurel on grey hairs is laid,
  Or on the combed tresses of the dead.

[BRITANNICUS *goes to the top of the stairs to recite, and at a
sign from* NERO *wine is handed to him.*

BRITANNICUS. This is too hot: some snow to cool it: so—
  [*Cold snow is put in and he drinks. He then recites.*
  Beside the melancholy surge I roam—
  A sad exile, a stranger, sick for home:
  A prince I was in my far native land

Who wander to and fro this alien sand:
Riches I had, and steeds, a glimmering crown;
Never had known a harshness or a frown.
Now must I limp and beg from door to door,
Wet with the storm, or in the sun footsore:
I, by a brother's cunning dispossessed,
Crave for these languid limbs a place of rest.
Pity me, robbed of all!

[*He gives a cry and falls headlong. His limbs quiver a moment and then are still. Meanwhile the shower of roses has slackened. There is a dead silence, and in the silence slowly all the guests turn and look at* NERO, *who rises, with the emerald in his eye.*

NERO. Lift up the prince and bear him to his room.
I do entreat that none of you will stir
Or rise perturbed: my brother, since his birth,
Was ever thus: the fit will pass from him.
Refill the cups: proceed we with the feast!

[*There is an attempt to renew the feasting, but soon a scene of uproar and confusion arises, and the guests leave the tables in alarm.*

[AGRIPPINA *alone remains unmoved, and then, as the guests have departed in disorder, she confronts* NERO *alone.*

AGRIPPINA. Thou hast done this.

NERO. Mother, I am thy son!

ACT III

SCENE I

SCENE. — NERO'S *private chamber. Enter* **NERO** *hastily and perturbed, followed by* **SENECA, BURRUS,** *and* **TIGELLINUS,** *his privy-councillors.*

BURRUS. Caesar, still glides the dead Britannicus
  About the palace, and his memory
  Your mother, Agrippina, uses: makes
  Out of his ghost a faction for herself.
  She grows a public peril; much you owe
  To her, but more to Rome; from Antium
  She rages disappointed to and fro.
  Me for your army you hold answerable,
  But can no longer if you suffer her
  To lure the legions from their loyalty.
  Her creatures whisper to your sentinels,
  Corrupt your officers, inflame your guards.
  A sullen silence on the camp is fallen,
  A word, and it will roar in mutiny.

TIGELLINUS. Everywhere steal her agents and her spies,
  Gliding through temples, baths, and theatres;
  Possess all angles, corners, noonday halts,
  And darknesses; they flit with casual poison
  Softly; the city secretly is filled
  With murmurs, lifted eyebrows, and with sighs.
  The mischief's in the very blood of Rome
  Unless the sore that feeds it is cut out.

NERO. Why, I myself have visited the fleet
  With Anicetus: sullen droop the sails
  Or flap in mutiny against the mast.
  Burdened with barnacles the untarred keels

Drowse on the tide with parching decks unswabbed,
And anchors rusting on inglorious ooze.
All indolent the vast armada tilts,
A leafless resurrection of dead trees.
The sailors in a dream do go about
Or at the fo'c's'le ominously meet.
Should any foe upon the sea-line loom
They'll light with ease upon an idle prey.
And yet I felt the grandeur of stagnation
And the magnificence of idleness.

BURRUS. She hath seduced the breast-plates and the sails.

NERO. [*Distracted.*] Here I pronounce her exile.

TIGELLINUS. Whither then?

ANICETUS. To Britain send her. There for Claudius
  I fought; a melancholy isle, alone,
  Sundered from all the world; and banned by God
  With separating, cold, religious wave,
  And haunted with the ghost of a dead sun
  Rising as from a grave, or all in blood
  Returning wounded heavily through mist.
  Her rotting peoples amid forests cower,
  Or mad for colour paint their bodies blue.
  There in eternal drippings of the leaf
  Or that dead summer of the living fly,
  And by the eternal sadness of the surf,
  Ambition cannot live, hope cannot breathe.
  Even the fieriest spirit there will rust
  Or gutter like a candle in the rain.
  To Britain send her.

TIGELLINUS. Never isle remote
  On the sad water, never desert sand
  In trembling flame, nor rock-built prison-house
  Shall tame her: there's the danger, that she lives.
  While she hath life, it is no matter where,
  While she hath breath, no other dares to breathe,

Not Caesar, even!

  NERO. This breath to her I owe.

TIGELLINUS. [*Cautiously and slowly watching
  NERO, as do the others.*] Caesar, there is a region of exile
  Whence none hath yet returned — your pardon, sir —

NERO. [*Starts and turns away.*] No, no, no!
  I remember very clear
  How gently she would wake me long ago.

BURRUS. Then be thy mother's son still and surrender
  This toy of Rome to her: she bought it you:
  Now, wearied, give it back!

NERO. Ah, patience, sir!
  I cannot in one moment gird myself
  To murder all these kisses, and she hath
  A vastness in this narrow world so rare,
  A sweep majestical about the earth —
  True, that she hath no ear for verse — —

  TIGELLINUS. For thine.

NERO. Yet passion, fury, and ambition, these
  Are primal things in our elaborate age.
  Ill can we spare them.

  BURRUS. Now, 'tis you or she.

NERO. A little time in which to fix my mind.
  I go to Baiae; for I am not housed
  Here as I should be: all the palace seems
  To me a hovel; scarcely can I breathe.
  I should be roofed with gold, and walled with gold,
  Should tread on gold; and if I cast mine eyes
  Over the city, they should view a scene
  Of spacious avenues and breathing trees,

And buildings plunged in odorous foliage.
This is a petty city: I have thought
It might be well to raze it to the ground
And build another and an ampler Rome,
More worthy site for this imperial soul.
I'll go to Baiae, there to dream this dream.

TIGELLINUS. Might I propose you go not all alone?
  At times the answering flash from other eyes
  Can aid the mightiest; and a woman's thought— —

  NERO. Yes—Yes—Poppaea!

  BURRUS. Otho will be jealous.

TIGELLINUS. And is already dangerous; he has joined
  The Agrippina faction.

NERO. He must be
  Promoted then to—Lusitania.

  TIGELLINUS. Thule were safer—still.

NERO. Here I appoint him
  Sole governor of Lusitania.
  To Baiae now—Poppaea—a new Rome!

  [*Exit* NERO.

TIGELLINUS. He hesitates—but I will see Poppaea:
  She can find means we cannot, and we thus
  Can use her beauty for our policy.

  [*Exeunt* TIGELLINUS, BURRUS, SENECA, *and* ANICETUS.

SCENE II

SCENE. — *The tiring chamber of* **POPPAEA** — *signs of luxury, implements of a Roman lady's toilet of the period.* **POPPAEA** *reclining, with a single maid.*

POPPAEA. Myrrha, more gold upon these builded curls.
  How often, child?

  MYRRHA. Mistress, forgive me.

  [*A slave has entered.*

  POPPAEA. Well?

  SLAVE. Mistress, the Emperor's minister, Tigellinus.

  [POPPAEA *signs* MYRRHA *to go.*

  Enter TIGELLINUS

TIGELLINUS. Lady, I am loth to interrupt this toil,
  But come on a secret errand.

  POPPAEA. Well, what is it?

TIGELLINUS. Long have I watched you, and to me it seemed
  You had some mighty wish within your soul
  As yet unspoken? Ah, I know it well.
  You would climb high, even to the very height?

  POPPAEA. [*Rising.*] I would.

  TIGELLINUS. You would be — mistress of the world?

  POPPAEA. Ah!

TIGELLINUS. And shall be: we aim at the same goal.
  You from ambition, I from policy.

  POPPAEA. Speak clearer.

TIGELLINUS. 'Tis our wish to free young Nero
  From Agrippina's dangerous dominance —

To free him of her quite. Now she too stands
In your own path. Your loveliness may work
Upon him: and we with policy the while —
Will you make cause with us?

POPPAEA. I understand.
  You need this beauty as an added bait
  To lure when policy can drive him not.
  What do I gain at last?

TIGELLINUS. The throne itself.
  Octavia is a shadow: cannot stand
  Between you and the world: but Agrippina,
  Never will suffer you while she has breath.

  POPPAEA. I will not tempt him to a mother's murder.

TIGELLINUS. Nor do we ask it: only that you draw
  His wandering fancy from her with a sweet
  Interposition of this loveliness,
  Free him of her, then bind him to yourself.

POPPAEA. I will attempt it. I will fly at it.
  I go to him to Baiae this same day.

  TIGELLINUS. Remember all the earth is in thy reach.

  [*Exit* TIGELLINUS.

  POPPAEA *claps her hands — enter various maids*

  POPPAEA. Lorilla, see, this henna is o'erdone.

  LORILLA. O pardon, mistress.

POPPAEA. And you, Lalage,
  My lips more brilliant.

  LALAGE. Yet — —

POPPAEA. Remember, child,
  That I walk ever veiled: what in the sun
  Glares, being veiled a finer richness takes
  And more provokes: how many struggling flies
  This veil, the web of mine, hath struggling held
  Which else were freed!

  [*Gazing at her face in mirror.*

  Ah! this left eyebrow — who?
  Who painted this?

  MAID. [*Trembling.*] I, madam.

POPPAEA. You are young:
  Else I would have you stripped and lashed till blood
  Flew from you.

  MAID. Mercy!

POPPAEA. Call old Lydia.
  Lydia, this eyebrow — the old touch.

LYDIA. My hands
  Tremble, but I'll essay.

POPPAEA. [*Gazing in mirror.*] So — that is well.
  Children, when there shall come, and come there must,
  The smallest marring wrinkle on this face,
  And come there must — our bodies fall like flowers,
  This face shall feel the ruin of the rose —
  When time, howe'er light, shall touch this cheek,
  Then quick farewell! Listen, I will not live
  Less lovely, nor this cruel beauty lose,
  And I perforce grow kind: I'll not survive
  The deep delicious poison of a smile
  Nor mortal music of the sighing bosom
  That slowly overcomes the fainting brain.
  It shall not dawdle downward to the grave;

I'll pass upon the instant of perfection.
No woman shall behold Poppaea fade:
And now to Baiae!

MYRRHA. Thence the Emperor
  Hath sent three messengers already.

POPPAEA. Ah!
  Blue Baiae, warm beside a sparkling sea
  Where I will win young Nero—and the world!

OTHO. The Emperor hath sent three messengers
  Demanding you for Baiae: yet am I
  Not asked: what means this lonely summons, wife?

  POPPAEA. Can you not trust me?

OTHO. When I gaze on you,
  'Yes'—when your voice is murmuring at my ear,
  'Yes'—but at times when I am pressed by crowds
  Or yearn alone beside the breaking wave— —

POPPAEA. Will you not trust me? Why then do I go?
  Is't for myself? You know well—'tis for you;
  To praise the Emperor's verses—but for you;
  To applaud his feeblest gesture—but for you;
  To coax from him a kingdom—but for you!
  Yet are you angered.

OTHO. 'Tis a perilous game.
  Nero may ask more of your loveliness.

POPPAEA. A woman may surrender inch by inch
  Even to the edge of shame: then sudden rise

Unmelting ice.

OTHO. Poppaea, I like it not.

POPPAEA. All is for you.

Enter an OFFICER *with* ATTENDANTS

OFFICER. Sir, from the Emperor.
  Thus Caesar saith: 'Hereby do we decree
  Otho, our bosom's friend, sole governor
  Of Lusitania: with imperial leave
  Whom to appoint, dismiss: all revenues
  In his control: thither let him proceed
  To-morrow ere sunset.'

OTHO. [*Looking at* POPPAEA, *then turning to* OFFICER.]
  I shall obey.

  [*Exit* OFFICER *and* OTHERS.

  Dismiss the slaves.

  POPPAEA. Otho, I swear — —

  OTHO. Dismiss them.

  POPPAEA. Myrrha, stay by me! On my knees I swear — —

  OTHO. Stand up! You knew this?

  POPPAEA. Dear, I never could — —

OTHO. [*Taking her by the arm.*] You go to Baiae into Caesar's arms.
  I am — promoted — to the ends of the earth,
  Anywhere, anywhere, so I be not there
  To interrupt.

  [*He throws her from him — snatches his dagger.*

POPPAEA. Kill me then if you will.
  Here — here! I will not flinch, so I die true.

You'll not suspect my corpse.

OTHO. It has been planned,
  Thought out, and timed—for in his deepest plot
  Our Nero has an eye for drama still.
  He hath imagined that which now we act.

  POPPAEA. Kill me—I love you! Ere you strike, one kiss.

  OTHO. Ah! [*Recoiling.*]

POPPAEA. But one kiss—a kiss of olden days,
  When we two were most happy: Caesar was not,
  And you had laughed at him! A harp-player,
  But not my man, my Otho! Think you I
  Who have had these arms about me, and these lips
  Burn up my own, could languish for a mime?
  I am a child—I have done wrong—forgive it—
  I sighed for thy advancement—speak to me!
  Now slap my hands or send me to my bed,
  I am a baby in these deep affairs.

OTHO. Go not to Baiae then: depart with me
  To Lusitania; words I'll count no more,
  But deeds—to Lusitania, come with me.

POPPAEA. Is it wise to disobey—is it wise, I ask?
  Set me aside, be mindful of yourself.

  OTHO. So you'll not come?

POPPAEA. For you alone I linger.
  I'll tarry but a little while behind you,
  And when I come, I'll greet you full of riches.

  OTHO. I dread to leave you in your loveliness.

  POPPAEA. Then I'll not go with you.

  OTHO. You will not—Why?

POPPAEA. Because you will not trust me. Show to me
  That you can trust me, Otho; and what joy,
  What satisfaction can you have to drag
  Your wife behind you, from dull jealousy
  Because you do not dare leave her behind
  For fear—I'll not be such a wife.

OTHO. Poppaea,
  No more I'll ask you to depart with me,
  I'll go alone: but this remember still—
  Gay have I been, a spendthrift and an idler,
  A brilliant fly that buzzed about the bloom.
  But I had that in me deep down, and still,
  Of which you, you alone, possess the key,
  A sullen nobleness to you disclosed
  E'en then with shame: and by no other guessed.
  This you well know: betray not that at least;
  For even the lightest woman here is scared,
  And dreads to dabble deeper in the soul.
  We have no children.

POPPAEA. [*Coming to him and putting up her face.*]
  Am I not child enough
  Who should be woman? You shall kiss these lips
  Once ere you go—so close they are to you.

  OTHO. The gods laugh out at me—but I must kiss you.

  POPPAEA. Can I not help your preparation?

OTHO. No.
  I shall not go with pomp; but as a soldier.

  POPPAEA. I think you are still angry?

OTHO. No! Farewell,
  I have brief time.

  POPPAEA. Ah! take me with you, then.

OTHO. What! You will come?

POPPAEA. I wish—I wish 'twere wise.
  My love shall bear your litter all the way.

   [*Exit* OTHO *hastily.*

   Re-enter MAID

MAID. Has he gone, lady? Had I such a man
  I could not let him part thus, not for Caesar.

POPPAEA. For Caesar! No: but Caesar means the world!
  For Baiae! The new gold-dust!

   MAID. Here, I have it.

   POPPAEA. Bear it yourself—entrust it to no other.

   [*Exeunt.*

SCENE III

NERO'S PRIVATE CHAMBER *in the villa at Baiae, looking directly upon the bay. Left, doors leading into the apartments. The water laps close up to the marble quay or terrace on which the action takes place. Right are seen prows of galleys at their moorings. Beyond is the curving shore of the bay, crowded with villas and temples. The scene is of extreme southern richness and serenity. Time noon*

   [NERO *is pacing restlessly to and fro. Enter a servant.*

   NERO. The lady Poppaea! Is she yet arrived?

   SERVANT. Sir, an hour since.

   NERO. [*Impatiently.*] Then why is she not here?

   [*Exit* SERVANT.

An hour since: yet she lingers while I ache
With passion. She comes not, still she delays.
To fly to her? No, 'twere unworthy of me — —
And yet, and yet — Ah! I must go to her.

Enter slaves bearing POPPAEA *on litter*

POPPAEA. [*Standing aloof and veiled.*]
  Caesar, by thee thrice summoned, I am here.
  What is your will?

  NERO. To have you at my side.

POPPAEA. Caesar, I am thy subject, and obeyed
  Unwillingly.

  NERO. Unwillingly?

POPPAEA. I come
  In loyalty: what service can I render?
  If none, then suffer me now to depart.
  I tremble to be seen with thee alone;
  No whisper yet has touched me.

NERO. So you come,
  But out of loyalty.

  POPPAEA. As fits thy subject.

  NERO. No, I am thine!

POPPAEA. Caesar, I will not hear,
  I must not if I would — that you know well.

  NERO. You come in cold obedience?

POPPAEA. I have said so.
  Yet — —

NERO. [*Eagerly.*] Well—well——

POPPAEA. Nero—nay, Caesar—my lord.

NERO. Nero, I'd have you say.

POPPAEA. That slipped from me—
  Is't treason? I know nothing of the laws.

NERO. You come because thrice summoned?

POPPAEA. In my mind
  There lurked another reason for my coming.

NERO. What then?

POPPAEA. A thought that like a captive bird
  I have kept warm about my heart so long
  I am loth to let it fly forth to the cold.

NERO. [*Approaching her.*] Tell me this thought.

POPPAEA. Then, Caesar, I have long
  Brooded upon the music of thy verse.
  It doth beset me—and, O pardon me,
  If, little fool that I am, I longed to speak
  But once alone with him who made it. Now,
  What have I said? I will return forthwith.

NERO. O not thy beauty moves me but thy mind!

POPPAEA. I think I have some little ear for verse.
  There is one line——

NERO. Yes—yes——

POPPAEA. Of burning Troy—
  'O city amorous red, thou flagrant rose'——

NERO. A regal verse! But the arm extended thus
  Toward doomed Ilium. Say on.

POPPAEA. My eyes
  Are filled with tears.

    NERO. Remove thy veil and weep.

POPPAEA. [*Starting back.*] For no man—save my husband—O my lord!
  He is despatched to Lusitania.

    NERO. Know you not why?

    POPPAEA. I know not—cannot guess.

    NERO. That he might stand no more between us two.

POPPAEA. O sir, he is my husband, and my way
  Is with him wheresoe'er he go. My duty——

    NERO. But your inclining?

POPPAEA. That I will not say.
  But Lusitania is henceforth my home.
  Nero, I will speak truth: I'll not deny
  There is some strange communion of the soul
  'Twixt you and me: but I'll not yield to this,
  No, nor shall you compel me, Caesar: I
  Will follow Otho even to banishment.
  There are more sacred things in my regard
  Than mutual pleasure from melodious verse.

    NERO. Nothing, when soul meets soul without alloy.

POPPAEA. I fear you do forget I am a woman.
  Dear to us before all are household cares.

    NERO. O to the average, not to thee.

    POPPAEA. Farewell!

NERO. You shall not go thus.

POPPAEA. Caesar, chain me here,
  But in neglected duty I shall pine.

NERO. [*Angrily striding to and fro.*] Ah!

POPPAEA. And imagine that he did not live—
  That I were free to indulge this panting soul—
  Still there are bars between us none can break.

NERO. You mean my wife Octavia?

POPPAEA. Well—and yet
  Not she, perhaps.

NERO. Who then? What other bars?

POPPAEA. Your mother Agrippina.

NERO. Still my mother!

POPPAEA. She would not bear it: would command her son
  To leave me: a younger woman has no hope
  Against her.

NERO. I am not her lackey.

POPPAEA. No?
  Ah, but her child, and born but to obey.
  And yet though wiser, mightier, than myself,
  You shall not find in her a listener
  So still, so answerable to your mood.
  And, I will say it, you'll not find in her
  One who has dived so deep into your soul,
  Who sees—I cannot flatter—sees that greatness
  Which she too long keeps under: were I you
  I would be Caesar, spite of twenty mothers,
  And seem the mighty poet that I am.
  I'll go.

NERO. You madden me — —

POPPAEA. Farewell again.

NERO. Poppaea, go not, go not. All the east
  Burns in me, and the desert fires my blood.
  I parch, I pine for you. My body is sand
  That thirsts. I die, I perish of this thirst,
  To slake it at your lips! You madden me.

  [*He seizes her cloak and she stands revealed.*

Goddess! What shall I give thee great enough?
I'll give thee Rome — I'll give thee this great world,
And all the builded empire as a toy.
The Mediterranean shall thy mirror be,
Thy jewels all sparkling stars of heaven.
The orb of the earth — throw it on thy lap
But for a kiss — one kiss!

  POPPAEA. But Agrippina?

  NERO. Agrippina?

POPPAEA. No — I'll not think of it!
  I'll have no violence for my sake committed.
  If by some chance unlooked for she should die,
  If in some far, far time she should succumb
  To creeping age — then — —

  NERO. Then?

  Enter MESSENGER *hurriedly*

MESSENGER. Sir, urgent business —
  The State demands you.

  NERO. [*Furiously.*] Pah! — the State!

POPPAEA. O Nero!
  Remember first the State — me afterward!

  NERO. Empress!

  [*He leads her out.*

  [*He returns and stands as in a dream while the* COUNCILLORS *enter.*

BURRUS. How long? How long, sir?
  Agrippina
  Is drawing to her net the dregs of Rome,
  Makes mutinous the rabble and the scum.

  [NERO *makes weary gesture.*

SENECA. And, sir, she has not scrupled to enroll
  The ragged, shrieking Christians, who wash not,
  The refuse of the empire, all that flows
  To this main sewer of Rome she counts upon.

TIGELLINUS. [*Stealing forward.*] And, sir, if
    these things move you not — a letter.

  NERO. [*Reading.*] 'I, Agrippina, daughter of Germanicus, of Claudius widow, of Nero mother, hereby do declare that though I have sat tame under private injuries, I will not forgo my public privileges, nor consent to be banished from high festival or ceremony. I purpose then to be present at Baiae at Minerva's feast, together with the Emperor, and will hold no second place. This is my ancient right and to that right I cleave. THE AUGUSTA.'

  SENECA. This is her ultimate audacity.

  TIGELLINUS. And this our utmost opportunity.

NERO. Sirs, seeing that the State demands this life,
  Seeing that I must choose 'twixt her and Rome,
  I do consent to Agrippina's death.
  The State like Nature must be pitiless,
  And I must ruthless be as Nature's Lord.
  But I'll be no Orestes, I'll not lift

This hand against her: see you then to that!
It is enough to have conceived this deed.
The how, the when, the where, I leave to you.

TIGELLINUS. She is delivered now into our hands,
  And runs into the toils we had not set.
  In Baiae no Praetorians are camped,
  No populace inflamed in her cause;
  A solitary woman doth she come.
  Caesar, receive her graciously and well.
  Smile all distrust away and speak her soft,
  While we devise for her a noiseless doom.

ANICETUS. Caesar, a sudden thought hath come to me.
  A pleasure pinnace lies in Baiae Bay
  Built for thyself: on this let her return
  In the deep night after Minerva's feast,
  Or supper given in sign of amity.
  I will contrive a roof weighted with lead
  Over the couch whereon she will recline.
  Once in deep water at a signal given
  The roof shall fall: and with a leak prepared
  The ship shall sink and plunge her in the waves.
  In that uncertain water what may chance?
  What may not? To the elements this deed
  Will be imputed, to a casual gust
  Or striking squall upon the moody deep.

NERO. Wonderful! This gives beauty to an act
  Which else were ugly and of me unworthy.
  So mighty is she that her proper doom
  Could come but by some elemental aid.
  Her splendid trouble asketh but the sea
  For sepulchre: her spirit limitless
  A multitudinous and roaring grave.
  Here's nothing sordid, nothing vulgar. I
  Consign her to the uproar whence she came.
  Be the crime vast enough it seems not crime.
  I, as befits me, call on great allies.

I make a compact with the elements.
And here my agents are the very winds,
The waves my servants, and the night my friend.

BURRUS. Suppose the night be clear, with a bright moon,
A calm sea.

NERO. On the moon I can rely.
Last night I wrote to her a glimmering verse;
She is white with a wan passion for my lips.
The moon will succour me. Depart from me—
Trouble me not with human faces now.

[*Exeunt* COUNCILLORS.

[*Meanwhile* POPPAEA *appears behind in a gorgeous dress with white arms extended against the curtains.*

SCENE IV

SCENE.—*The same—glittering starlight*

Enter various servants bearing wine-jars and dishes from the inner suf-fer-room, in procession. Then BURRUS, SENECA, ANICETUS, *and* TIGELLINUS

BURRUS. 'Tis not man's work to witness this. I have fought
Neck-deep in blood and spared not when the fit
Was on me, but I cannot gaze on this.
Have you a heart, old man?

TIGELLINUS. No, not in hours
Like these: the brain is all. I fear, I fear him
The last farewell—he will not bear it out!

SENECA. How to excuse my soul, yet I am here.
Was this mere acting, or a true emotion?

ANICETUS. A little of both, but most, I fear it, true.

TIGELLINUS. Is all prepared and timed? No hazard left?

ANICETUS. Yonder the barge with lights and fluttering flags.
  The canopy whereunder Agrippina
  Will sit is heavily weighted: at a sign
  A bolt withdrawn will launch it on her head.

  Enter NERO

NERO. I cannot do it: if she goes, she goes.
  I cannot say farewell, and kiss her lips,
  Ere I commit her body to the deep.

TIGELLINUS. All hangs upon the fervour of farewell,
  The kiss, the soft word, and the hand detained,
  All hangs on it; go back.

  NERO. 'Tis difficult.

  [NERO *turns. Enter* AGRIPPINA.

  Come out into the cool a moment, mother.

AGRIPPINA. This seemeth like to old days come again,
  Evenings of Antium with a rising moon.

  [*Stroking his hair*.

My boy, my boy, again! Look in my eyes.
So as a babe would you look up at me
After a night of tossing, half-awake,
Blinking against the dawn, and pull my head
Down to you, till I lost you in my hair.
Do you remember many a night so thick
With stars as this—you would not go to bed,
But still would paddle in the warm ocean
Spraying it with small hands into the skies.

NERO. Yes, I remember.

AGRIPPINA. Or when you would sail
 In a slight skiff under a moon like this,
 Though chidden oft and oft.

NERO. Ah! I recall it.

AGRIPPINA. A wilful child—the sea—ever the sea—
 Your mother could not hold you from the sea.
 Will you be sore if I confess a thought?

NERO. Ah! no, mother!

AGRIPPINA. So foolish it seems now.
 Awhile I doubted whether I should come.

NERO. Why, then?

AGRIPPINA. Now, do not laugh at me—I say
 You will not laugh at me?

NERO. No!

AGRIPPINA. Why—I thought
 That you perhaps would kill me if I came!
 Truly I did!

NERO. I kill you!

AGRIPPINA. 'O,' I said,
 'I have wearied him: he is weary of his mother.'

NERO. Oh!

AGRIPPINA. In my ears there buzzed that prophecy—
 'Nero shall reign but he shall kill his mother.'

[NERO *starts.*

AGRIPPINA. Now—now—I had not told you had I not
  Been above measure happy. Now no more
  Wild words, no more mad words between us two,
  Who all the while are aching to be friends.
  O how your hands come waxen once again
  Within my own: again behind your voice
  The hesitating tardy bird-like word
  And the sweet slur of 'r's.' O but to-night
  Even grandeur palls, the splendid goal: to-night
  I am a woman and am with my child.

    [*A pause and she strains him to her.*

  Beautiful night that gently bringest back
  Mother to son, and callest all thy stars
  To watch it. Quiet sea that bringest peace
  Between us two. Hast thou not thought how still
  The air is as with silent pleasure? Child,
  Is not the night then more than common calm?

    NERO. A sparkling starlight and a windless deep.

AGRIPPINA. Never until to-night did I so feel
  The lure of the sea that lures me to lie down
  At last after such heat. Ah, but the stars
  Are falling and I feel the unseen dawn.
  Son, I must go at once. Where is my maid
  To wrap me? Sweet and warm now is the night
  And I am glad I had prepared to go
  By water, not by land.

    Enter SERVANT, *hurriedly*

    SERVANT. O Caesar!

    NERO. Well?

SERVANT. Thy mother's galley by a random barge
  Was struck, and now is sinking fast.

AGRIPPINA. Alas!
  Now must I go by land.

  NERO. Yes, go by land.

  [TIGELLINUS *signals to* ANICETUS.

ANICETUS. Yonder there lies a barge with fluttering flags,
  A gilded pinnace, a light pleasure-boat
  Built for you with much art and well designed.
  Will you return in her? Easily she
  Can swing round to the landing-stage.

AGRIPPINA. Yes — yes —
  I'll go in her — Why not?

  NERO. It was foretold — —

  Enter ACCERONIA, *who elaborately wraps* AGRIPPINA

AGRIPPINA. Nero, my maid a moment to enwrap me.
  As the wrapping is finished.
  I have slept ill of late: but I shall have
  A soft and steady breeze across the bay.
  I shall sleep sound. Now, Nero, now good-bye.
  For ever we are friends?

  NERO. Good-bye: yet stay!

  [*During this dialogue he is continually detaining her.*

  Have I been kind, this last hour? Say.

  AGRIPPINA. Most kind.

NERO. You have no need to go this moment — one
  More moment of thee, mother.

AGRIPPINA. You shall see me
  To-morrow. Will you cross the bay to me,
  Or shall I come to you?

NERO. I'll come to you
  To-morrow! Ah! to-morrow! But to-night.
  Now let me have you once more in my arms.
  [*Detaining her.*
  Is old Cynisca with you still?

  AGRIPPINA. [*Going.*] She is.

  NERO. Stay, stay, give her this ring: she nursed me.

AGRIPPINA. Yes.
  I see you have my amulet.

  NERO. O yes.

AGRIPPINA. So bright the night you'll see me all the way
  Across the shining water.

  NERO. [*Clinging to her.*] O farewell!

AGRIPPINA. [*Descends to water.*]
  Good-night, child! I shall see you then to-morrow.
  Already it hath dawned.

  NERO. Mother, good-night.

  [*Exit* AGRIPPINA.

TIGELLINUS. [*To crew in barge.*]
  Strike up the music there, a joyous strain!
  And sing, you boatmen; the Augusta comes.

  [*Sounds of joyful music are heard, and singing, as the pinnace
  puts off with measured beat of oars.*

NERO. It hath put off: she hath gone: she sitteth happy.
  See, the dead woman waves her hand to me.

Now the bark turns the headland.

ANICETUS. But will soon
  Steal into sight, well out upon the bay.

  TIGELLINUS. Caesar, let none deny thou art an actor.

NERO. [*Passionately.*] Was I all actor then?
  That which I feigned
  I felt, and when it was my cue to kiss her,
  The whole of childhood rushed into the kiss.
  When it was in my part to cling about her,
  I clung about her mad with memories.
  The water in my eyes rose from my soul,
  And flooding from the heart ran down my cheek.
  Did my voice tremble? Then it trembled true
  With human agony behind the art.
  Gods! What a scene!

  TIGELLINUS. Listen!

ANICETUS. She is well out,
  Glassed in the bay with all her lights and flags.
  Soon will a crash and cry come in our ears.

NERO. [*Going out.*] How calm the night when I would have it wild!
  Aloof and bright which should have rushed to me
  Hither with aid of thunder, screen of lightning!
  I looked for reinforcement from the sky.
  Arise, you veiling clouds; awake, you winds,
  And stifle with your roaring human cries.
  Not a breath upon my cheek! I gasp for air.
  [*To* OTHERS.] Do you suppose the very elements
  Are conscious of the workings of this mind?
  So careful not to seem to share my guilt?
  Yet dark is the record of wind and wave;
  This ocean that creeps fawning to our feet
  Comes purring o'er a million wrecks and bones.
  If the cold moon hath sinned not, she hath been privy.

She aids me not, but watches quietly.
A placid sea, still air, and bright starlight.

ANICETUS. But Caesar, see, a gradual cloud hath spread
  Over the moon; the ship's light disappears.
  She is vanished.

  NERO. She is veiled from sight.

TIGELLINUS. My eyes
  Can find her not; she is enwrapped in mist.

  SENECA. A dimness and no more.

  BURRUS. And silence.

NERO. Hush!
  How wonderful this waiting and this pause.
  Could one convey this in the theatre?
  This deep suspense, this breathlessness? Perhaps.
  The air weighs on the brain— —what sound was that?

  TIGELLINUS. Nothing, sir.

  NERO. In this thrill a leaf would thunder.

  [*A pause.*

I never noted so exactly how
The shadow of that cypress falls aslant
Upon the dark bank yonder.

  BURRUS. Would it were over!

NERO. Feel you no shuddering pleasure in this pause?
  But me this fraught expectancy allures;
  The tingling stillness, for each moment now
  The crash, a cry, may come, but it comes not.

  TIGELLINUS. Anicetus, have you bungled?

[*A cry is heard far off, and a crash, then silence.*

NERO. It is done.
  I cannot look: peer seaward, one of you —
  What do you see?

  SENECA. Darkness, and veiled stars.

NERO. Is there no shimmer of a floating robe?
  Pierce through the darkness!

  BURRUS. Nothing visible.

NERO. I seem to see her lying amid shells,
  And strange sea-things come round her wondering,
  Inspecting her with cold and rheumy eyes.
  The water sways her helpless up and down.

  BURRUS. Caesar, you have no further need of me?

  NERO. [*Dreamily.*] No, sir.

  BURRUS. Good-night, and pleasant be thy dreams.

  SENECA. Or me?

  NERO. No, no!

SENECA. At least bear witness, sir,
  I had no hand in this: but was compelled,
  A loth spectator, to behold thy deed!

  ANICETUS. Caesar, you'll not forget the service done?

NERO. Never shall I forget thee, Anicetus.
  Leave me alone.

  [*Exeunt all but* TIGELLINUS, *who creeps back again.*

TIGELLINUS. Sole master of the world!
  Caesar at last: the Emperor of the earth,
  Now thou art free — to write immortal verse,
  To give thy genius wing, to strike the stars.

And thou hast made this tragic sacrifice,
Slaying what is most dear, most close to thee,
To give thy being vent and utterance.
Apollo shall reward thee for this deed.

NERO. Go to thy room, old man, and—wilt thou sleep?

TIGELLINUS. Already I am drowsing; early then
To-morrow I will come to you.

NERO. Good-night.

TIGELLINUS. Caesar, good-night.

[*Exit* TIGELLINUS.

[*Thunder heard.*

NERO. Ah! thunder! thou art come
At last, too late! What catches at my heart?
I—I—her boy, her baby that was, even I
Have killed her: where I sucked there have I struck.
Mother! Mother! [*He drinks.*
The anguish of it hath taken hold of me,
And I am gripped by Nature. O, it comes
Upon me, this too natural remorse.
I faint! I flinch from the raw agony!
I cannot face this common human throe!
Ah! Ah! the crude stab of reality!
I am a son, and I have killed my mother!
Why! I am now no more than him who tills
Or reaps: and I am seized by primal pangs.
Mother! [*He drinks.*
The thunder crieth motherless.
Ah! how this sword of lightning thrusts at me!
O, all the artist in my soul is shattered,
And I am hurled into humanity,
Back to the sweat and heart-break of mankind.
I am broken upon the jagged spurs of the earth.
I can no more endure it. Mother!

[*He drinks again, walking distractedly to and fro, not looking se-award. But as he at last turns, slowly out from the sea appears the figure of* AGRIPPINA *with dripping hair, who comes slowly towards him in silence.*

[*He cries aloud and falls in a swoon. She comes and looks at him.*

AGRIPPINA. Child!

[*She stoops, removes the amulet from his arm, flings it into the sea, and passes out in silence.*

SCENE V

SCENE.—*The same. Dawn breaking;* NERO *discovered lying in a swoon*

NERO. [*Slowly.*] Dawn! In the night o'er-past a lightning flash!
  Ah! I remember—here my mother's ghost
  Stood—on this very ground—I feel the air
  Still cold from her—and here the lightning burned.
  So I awake my mother's murderer.
  That was her ghost that stole on me sea-marred,
  Silent—the ocean falling from her hair.

  Enter TIGELLINUS

  TIGELLINUS. Caesar at last! Sole master of the world!

NERO. O Tigellinus, in the mid of night,
  The spirit of my whelmed mother stole
  Hither upon me, dumb out of the deep.
  Heaven gave a flash: I saw her face and fell.

TIGELLINUS. Her spirit! Better that than she herself.
  Dismiss dark fancies now—this day thou art free.

74

NERO. No, but enthralled by her for ever-more.
  She is my air, my ocean, and my sky.

TIGELLINUS. The night has wrought this sickly mood on you —
  Natural — it will pass.

NERO. Never, O never!
  You flatter, you console, you would assuage,
  But you are human, can forget and change.
  But yonder rocky coast remembers yet.
  That countenance changes not: that conscious bay
  Maintains its everlasting memory.
  This privy region saw, and it shall see
  For ever what was done. The amulet!
  Filched from me! Was it then a ghost I saw?

Enter SEAMAN *hurriedly, followed by* BURRUS

SEAMAN. Caesar, my news must plead for this intrusion.
  I was aboard the ship whereon the Augusta
  Set sail: when the roof fell, thy mother's maid
  Cried 'Save me! I am the Emperor's mother!'
  Straight
  Crushed under many a blow, she dropped and died.
  But silently thy mother Agrippina
  Slid from the ship into the water and swam
  Shoreward. With white and jewelled arms she thrust
  Out through the waves and lay upon the foam.
  We heard her through the ripple breathing deep,
  And when we heard no more, we watched her still —
  Her hair behind her blowing into gold
  As she did glimmer o'er the gloomy deep;
  And all the stars swam with her through the heavens,
  The hurrying moon lighted her with a torch,
  The sea was loth to lose her, and the shore
  Yearned for her; till we lost her in the dark,

Save now and then some splendid leap of the head.

  NERO. You know not if she be alive or dead?

  SEAMAN. Caesar, rejoice—thy mother lives.

  NERO. She lives?

SEAMAN. When I at last touched shore, I spoke with two
  Night-wandering fishermen. These two, it seems,
  Had borne her in their boat across the bay
  To her own villa.

NERO. [*Falling hysterically on neck of* SEA-MAN.]
  I am no murderer then!

TIGELLINUS. Have you considered, sir, what now may urge
  Thy mother, Agrippina, knowing all,
  Seeing that by no chance or accident
  Or sudden flurry of the ocean floor
  The ship collapsed. Safe is she, but how long?
  Will she not burst upon us suddenly?
  Sir, she must die to-night.

NERO. I'll not attempt
  A second time that life the sea restored;
  She is too vast a spirit to surprise.
  Even Nature stood aloof— —
  My mother shall be gloriously caged,
  Imprisoned in purple and immured in gold.
  In some magnificent captivity
  Worthy the captive let her day decline.

  [*Shouts without: enter* BURRUS.

BURRUS. Caesar, great news I bring: the Armenian
  Lies helpless on Tigranocerta's plain
  O'erwhelmed by Corbulo, and the huge host
  Dissolved. Armenia lies beneath your feet:

Rome yearns to welcome you.

NERO. To Rome I go
  Free-souled and guiltless of a mother's blood,
  Resume the accustomed feast, the race, the song,
  And I shall be received with public joy
  And clamour of congratulating Rome.

  [*Great cheering without: exit* NERO.

  [*A pause.*

TIGELLINUS. Burrus, she'll strike at us whate'er the cost:
  She'll slay the ministers if not the master.

  BURRUS. We are both dead unless some sudden scheme—

  Enter ANICETUS *at back*

  [*Turning.*] Here is another doomed as we ourselves.

TIGELLINUS. Ah, Anicetus! Agrippina lives,
  And she will launch her vengeance on us three,
  But first on you; you first set Nero on—
  You first proposed the scheme. You on the sea
  Bungled—Now on the land retrieve the error.
  To you we look.

  Enter POPPAEA *from behind and stands listening*

ANICETUS. My error is repaired
  Already. I first heard the Augusta lived,
  And instantly despatched a faithful troop
  To slay her at her villa o'er the bay.

  TIGELLINUS. How shall we know if they have found and slain
her?

ANICETUS. All this I have arranged and clearly planned.
  If they shall find that she hath fled to Rome,

Hark for one trumpet-call across the bay:
If they have found her at the villa, then
Hark for two trumpet-calls across the bay:
If they have found her and have slain her, then
Hark for three trumpet-calls across the bay!

   [*A burst of music without, and sounds of advancing procession.*

[*Enter soldiers and satellites, with attendants bearing a litter.
Lastly* NERO.

TIGELLINUS. Now as a conqueror in triumphant vein
  Ride through the thundering ways of risen Rome,
  Anticipating the Armenian car.

NERO. [*Ascending litter.*]
  Set out for Rome! And you, accusing coasts,
  Accuse no more. Guiltless I say farewell,
  And with a light heart journey toward Rome
  Joyous I go, for Agrippina lives.

   [*A great triumphal shout swells up again, and to the sound of military
music,* NERO *and the procession pass off. Meanwhile* TIGELLINUS *is
left in a listening attitude.* POPPAEA *stands breathless at back. There is a
pause. Then a trumpet-call is heard far off; a second; and a third.*
POPPAEA *rushes to* TIGELLINUS *and clasps his hand.*

ACT IV

SCENE I

SCENE. — *A tower overlooking Rome*

Enter SENECA, BURRUS, *and* PHYSICIAN

SENECA. How dark the future of the Empire glooms!

BURRUS. Now the Gaul mutters: the Praetorians
  Sullenly snarl.

SENECA. The Christians privily
  Conspire.

  BURRUS. The legions waver and whisper too.

  SENECA. [*To* PHYSICIAN.] What of the Emperor?

PHYSICIAN. Through Campania
  He rushes: and distracted to and fro
  Would fly now here, now there; behind each woe
  He sees the angered shade of Agrippina.
  Now hearing that Poppaea sinks toward death.
  Hither is he fast hurrying.

SENECA. Ah, Poppaea,
  No sooner Empress made than she must die — —

  BURRUS. See: she is carried hither.

SENECA. Here to look
  Her last upon the glory of the earth.

  [*Exeunt* SENECA, BURRUS, *and* PHYSICIAN.

[POPPAEA *enters, supported by handmaids. She takes a long look*
at Rome, then is assisted down to couch.

POPPAEA. Give me the glass again: beautiful yet!
  This face can still endure the sunset glow,
  No need is there for me to sue the shadow,
  Perfect out of the glory I am going.

  MYRRHA. Lady, the mood will pass: still you are young.

POPPAEA. Why comes not Nero near me?
  O he loathes
  Sickness or sadness or the touch of trouble,

MYRRHA. Nay, lady; hither he is riding fast,
  In fury spurring from Campania,
  And trouble upon trouble falls on him —
  Misfortune follows him like a faithful hound.

POPPAEA. I snared him, Myrrha, once; let him flutter away!
  But to relinquish the wide earth at last,
  And flit a faint thing by a shadowy river,
  Or yearning without blood upon the bank — —
  The loneliness of death! To go to strangers —
  Into a world of whispers — —

  [*Looking at and lifting her hair.*

                And this hair
  Rolling about me like a lighted sea
  Which was my glory and the theme of the earth,
  Look! Must this go? The grave shall have these eyes
  Which were the bliss of burning Emperors.
  After what time, what labour the high gods
  Builded the body of this beauty up!
  Now at a whim they shatter it! More light!
  I'll catch the last of the sun.

Enter SLAVE

SLAVE. Mistress, below
  The lady Acte stands and asks to see you.

POPPAEA. Come to inspect me fading: I fear not.
  Even a woman's eyes I need not shun.
  Bring her. [*Exit* SLAVE.
  Now, Myrrha, watch her hungering eyes.

Enter ACTE, *ushered by* SLAVE

POPPAEA. [*Vehemently.*] Take Nero! I am dying.

ACTE. Ah, not yet!

POPPAEA. I am dying. But you shall not hold him long——
  O, do not think it. Can you queen his heart?
  Can you be storm a moment, sun the next?
  A month, a long day under open skies,
  Would find your art exhausted, ended. I!
  I was a hundred women in an hour,
  And sweeter at each moment than them all.
  Why, I have struck him in the face and laughed.

ACTE. I love him: that concerns not him, nor you.
  A different goal I would have sought for him,
  A garment not of purple, but of peace.

POPPAEA. Of peace! Ha, ha!

ACTE. Vain now—I know it, vain.
  But if your words are true, and death is on you,
  Let us two at the least be friends at last.

POPPAEA. I bear no rancour—and yet if I dreamed
  That I was leaving you upon his bosom—
  But no: let there be peace between us two.

[ACTE *comes and kisses her.*

Your kiss falls kind upon my loneliness.
But, Acte, to let go of glory thus—
For I have drunk of empire, and what cup
Afterward can you offer to these lips?

ACTE. Of late there has been stealing on my mind
  A strange hope—a new vision.

POPPAEA. What is this?

ACTE. Do not laugh out at me: a sect despised—
  The Christians, tell us of an after life,
  A glory on the other side the grave.
  If there should be a kingdom not of this world,
  A spirit throne, a city of the soul!

POPPAEA. I want no spirit kingdom after death.
  The splendid sun, the purple, and the crown,
  These I have known, and I am losing them.

ACTE. Yet if the sun, the purple, and the crown
  Were but the shadows of another sun,
  Splendider—a more dazzling diadem?

POPPAEA. These can I see at least, and feel, and hear.

ACTE. Yes, with a mortal touch that falters now.

POPPAEA. [*Sobbing.*] O Acte, to be dumb, and deaf, and blind!

ACTE. Or live again with more transcendent sense,
  Hearing unchecked, and unimpeded sight.
  If we who walk now, then should wing the air,
  Who stammer now, then should discard the voice,
  Who grope now, then should see with other sight,
  And send new eyes about the universe.

POPPAEA. O, this is madness!

ACTE. Is it? Is it? Well—
  Yet have I heard this ragged people speak,
  And they have stirred me strangely: life they scorn,
  And yearn for death's tremendous liberty,
  But I—I cannot speak; yet I believe
  There is a new air blowing on the world,
  And a new budding underneath the earth.

POPPAEA. Ah, ah! the sun! The sun! It goeth down,
  How cold it grows: the night comes down on me.
  I'll have no lamp: but hold my hand in thine.

  ACTE. Sister, forget the world, it passeth.

  POPPAEA. [*Falling back.*] Rome!

SCENE II

SCENE.—*The same.* **SENECA, BURRUS, ACTE, *and* PHYSICIAN**

PHYSICIAN. The Emperor comes from gazing on Poppaea.
  What woe may that dead face not work on him,
  After such rain of dark calamities!

  SENECA. Why hath he summoned me?

PHYSICIAN. He knows not why.
  The infatuate orgies in Campania,
  Defeat, revolt, have wrought upon his mind,
  Till it begins to reel—behind each woe
  He sees the angered shade of Agrippina.

[*Enter* NERO *with tablets, murmuring to himself. He comes
to the* COUNCILLORS, *gazes at them, and retires to parapet.*

'Beautiful on her bed Poppaea lay'—
I have begun to write her epitaph.

[*He again gazes over parapet, murmuring to himself. Then turning*

Ah, blow supreme! Ah, ultimate injury!
I can no longer write: my brain is barren.
My gift, my gift, thou hast left me. Let me die!
Ah! what an artist perishes in me.

[*He again returns to parapet, gazing and murmuring, and throws
his tablets from him.*

Dead Agrippina rages unappeased.
At night I hear the trailing of a robe,
And the slain woman pauses at my door.
O! she is mightier having drunk of death;
Now hath she haled Poppaea from my arms;
Last doth she quench the holy fire within me— —

Enter MESSENGER

MESSENGER. Caesar, I bring dark news:
  Boadicea the British Queen is risen,
  And like a fire is hissing through the isle,
  Londinium and Camulodunum
  In ashes lie; the loosed barbarians
  In madness rage and ravish, murder and burn.

  BURRUS. Caesar, despatch.

  [*Brings* NERO *paper.*

NERO. Ah, this is still the deed
  Of Agrippina. Listen! Did ye not hear
  The rustle of a robe? [*Starting up.*
          Ah! thou art come!
I—I no order gave! Then did the brine
Drop from thy hair: but now blood falls from thee;
There, where they struck thee, once did I sleep sound.
What shall I do to appease thee? Let me die
Rather than see that wonder on thy face,

84

And stare on me of terrible surprise.
Thou com'st upon me!

   ACTE. Ah! what ails your mind?

   NERO. She is gone! The red drops those that fell from her!

   ACTE. Lo! I am with thee!

   NERO. Thou! And who art thou?

Enter in great haste an OFFICER, *followed by* OTHERS

OFFICER. Caesar, Rome burns! We cannot fight the fire
  Which blazes and consumes. How it arose
  None knows and none can tell. What shall we do?

ANOTHER. It sprung in the Suburra: whether lit
  By accident, dropped torch, or smouldering brand — —

   ANOTHER. Or by design — —

ANOTHER. Caesar, the Christians,
  Who hate the human race, have done this thing:
  They loathe thy rule and would abolish thee,
  And with thee, Rome.

ANOTHER. They have a prophecy
  That now the world is ending, and in fire
  The globe shall shrivel, and this empire fall
  In cinders.

   ANOTHER. And the moon be turned to blood.

NERO. The moon be turned to blood! But that is fine!
  These Christians have imaginations then!
  The moon in blood, and burning universe!
  Why, I myself might have conceived that scene!

OFFICER. Caesar, what shall be done?
  Still spreads the fire!
  A quarter of Rome in ashes lies already,
  And like a blackened corpse: and screaming mothers,
  Hugging their babes, dash through the fearful flames,
  And old men totter gasping through the blaze
  Or fall scorched to the ground. Stifled with smoke
  The population from their houses reel.
  Meantime the Christians, prophesying woe
  And final doom upon a wicked world,
  Hither and thither run, and with their dark
  Forebodings madden all the minds of men.
  To thee they point! To thee, the source of fire,
  Who has drawn down on them celestial flame.

  NERO. Magnificent! The aim of heavenly fire!

ANOTHER. They say the world shall crumble, and the skies
  Fall, and their God come in the clouds of heaven
  To judge the earth!

ANOTHER. But we are wasting breath
  Over the Christians: what now shall be done?
  To thee, Caesar, to thee, we come: for thou
  Alone mayst with this conflagration cope.

NERO. Listen! Did ye not hear a wailing then?
  The wailing of a woman in her grave?
  Again! A wailing, and I know the voice!

Enter OTHERS *hastily*

MESSENGER. Caesar, the fire has reached the Palatine!
  Rome will be ashes soon.

ANOTHER. We have fought fire
  With water: matched the elements in vain,
  For the fire triumphs: Caesar, what aid from thee?

    Enter ANOTHER

MESSENGER. Caesar, the temple of Jupiter is aflame.
  The shrine of Vesta next will crash to the earth.

   ANOTHER. Open the sluices of the Campus Martius.

   ANOTHER. Issue some sudden edict: give command.

NERO. No edict will I issue, or command.
  Let the fire rage.

   CHORUS. O Caesar!

   NERO. Let it rage!

ANOTHER. Caesar, 'tis said this fire was lit by thee.
  That thou wouldst burn old Rome to build a new,
  A Rome more glorious issuing from the flames:
  This tale hath maddened all the common folk
  Who, from their smouldering homes, curse thee aloud.

NERO. This fire is not the act of mortal mind,
  But is the huge conception of a spirit
  Dreaming beyond the tomb a mighty thought.
  She would express herself in burning fire:
  This is the awful vengeance of the dead;
  This is my mother Agrippina's deed.
  I will not baulk the fury of her spirit.
  No! Let her glut her anger on the city,
  For only Rome in ashes can appease her,
  Let the fire rage and purge me of her blood!
     [*The flame flashes upward.*
  Rage!
  Rage on!

See, see!
    How beautiful!
Like a rose magnificently burning!
        [*The flame flashes up.*
    Rage on!
Thou art that which poets use,
    Or which consumes them.
    Thou art in me!
Thou dreadful womb of mighty spirits,
    And crimson sepulchre of them!
        [*The flame flashes up.*
    Blaze! Blaze!
How it eats and eats!
    How it drinks!
What hunger is like unto the hunger of fire?
What thirst is like unto the thirst of flame?
        [*The flame flashes up.*
    O fury superb!
O incurable lust of ruin!
    O panting perdition!
    O splendid devastation!
    I, I, too, have felt it!
    To destroy — to destroy!
To leave behind me ashes, ashes.
        [*The flame flashes up.*
    Rage! Rage on!
Or art thou passion, art thou desire?
    Ah! terrible kiss!
        [*The flame flashes up.*
Now hear it, hear it!
A hiss as from mighty serpents,
  The dry, licking, wicked tongues!
Wouldst thou sting the earth to death?
    What a career!
  To clasp and devour and kill!
  To dance over the world as a frenzied dancer
With whirling skirts of world-wide flame!
        [*The flame flashes up.*
    Blaze! Blaze!

Or art thou madness visible,
Insanity seizing the rolling heavens.
    [*He points up.*
Thou, Thou, didst create the world
  In the stars innumerably smiling.
Thou art life, thou art God, thou art I!
     [*The flame flashes up.*
  Mother! Mother!
 This is thy deed.
  Hist! Hist! can you not see her
   Stealing with lighted torch?
She makes no sound, she hath a spirit's tread.
    Hast thou sated thy vengeance yet?
    Art thou appeased?
    [*The flame flashes up.*
 Be satisfied with nothing but the world,
   The world alone is fuel for thee.
   Mother!
   [*The flame flashes up.*
And I! See what a fire I have given thee,
  Rome for a funeral couch!
Had Achilles a pyre like to this
  Or had Patroclus?
Had they mourners such as I give to thee,
  Bereaved mothers and babes?
Now let the wailing cease from thy tomb,
  Here is a mightier wail!
Now let the haunting trumpet be dumb!

  ACTE. Nero!

NERO. Blaze! Rage! Blaze!
     [*The flame flashes up more fervently.*
For now am I free of thy blood,
I have appeased and atoned,
Have atoned with cries, with crashings, and with flaming.
Thy blood is no more on my head;
I am purged, I am cleansed;
I have given thee flaming Rome for the bed of thy death!

O Agrippina!

[*He falls in a swoon* — ACTE *runs towards him.*